Praise for Tak Lo and *I, Leader*

This book has lots of great insights, along with Tak's life learning experiences, which would be most beneficial for first-time founders, Ph.Ds/MBAs, and people who have recently joined or vstarted VC funds or accelerators. It contains guidance on how to build an accelerator, what founders need from mentors, advisors, and investors, and what they need to pay attention to in the early days of their startup journeys.

Naoki Kamimaeda

Partner at Global Brain & former Sony AI engineer

Tak, my esteemed friend, stands as both a great community builder and an AI expert. His critical book is a guiding beacon for those embarking on the AI gold rush of the 21st Century. Much like a seasoned coach, Tak meticulously lays out a winning game plan for startups, especially those venturing into the realm of AI exploration. Within its pages, he unveils the pivotal factors that have shaped the ascent of AI and provides invaluable insights on impact investment strategies.

Dr Chung Wai Keung, David

Chief Impact Officer, ImpactD, Former Cyberport CTO and Former Under Secretary, Innovation Technology and Industry Bureau, HKSAR Government

As the old saying goes, it's about the journey not just the destination. And in our world where the only certainty is change and where possibilities are endless, this book, which by definition has an end, captures the essence of infinity.

Another word for innovation is change, and for those that dare to dream and challenge the status quo and set out on the path least taken, this book is for you. Good luck on whatever you're building that is eating world."

Ben Son

Founder and Advisor

Tak is a polymath, and he sees the future. Not just tech, but tech, science, geopolitics, climate change and more— all at the same time, and the nonlinear interactions among them. He was super-early in AI, network state, and more. How can you be early? How do you see the future? What do you do with that vision? How can you be effective in executing? This book contains Tak's brilliant perspective on these questions. Every builder and investor would be wise to read it.

Trent McConaghy

Founder of Ocean Protocol and Ocean Predictoor, at the intersection of AI and Web3

At first, I was skeptical of the journal time jump format, but as I progressed, it became clear how effectively Tak makes it work. Tak's insights on leadership, teamwork, and responsibility, drawn from his army experience and building Zeroth, are incredibly impactful. The book is a compelling read that offers valuable lessons for aspiring leaders.

Vaisagh Viswanathan

CEO & Co-founder of Impress.ai, ex-Zeroth founder

Tak Lo is in the AI arena and shares well his insights into innovation leadership.

Robert Scoble

American blogger, technical evangelist, and author

I've turned to Tak Lo multiple times to understand the companies and technologies he's advised. As you'll see in this book, what makes him remarkable is that he's not just deeply immersed in mentoring and supporting the startups he's involved with. He's equally obsessed with leveling up his understanding by learning from others.

Andrew Warner

Founder of Mixergy & Bradford & Reed, and author of *Stop Asking Questions*

I've known Tak for over a decade and he was in AI before it was cool. I've seen and worked with him as a startup operator and investor. Through that and his military experience, he brings a clear headed perspective on business and leadership. His book distills all the lessons for startup founders everywhere.

Marvin Liao

Partner, Diaspora Ventures; CIO, Sukna Holdings

Tak's narrative is a clarion call to support the trailblazers of technology, those exceptional startups poised to bring about radical transformations in the societal fabric, rather than mere incremental changes. His book delves deep into the heart of AI's promise, spotlighting his relentless pursuit to invest in innovations that fundamentally redefine our way of life and what it means to be human.

Kenneth Lau

Comfiknit founder

Tak is the complete embodiment of give before you get. His passion for the founder community is matched only by his passion for the military veteran entrepreneur ecosystem. His experience and wisdom should be required reading for any founder thinking about taking the plunge into entrepreneurship. Required!

Josh Carter

Startup ecosystem builder/serial founder

As a serial entrepreneur and a participant in Zeroth's Z04 batch, my journey with Tak has extended from mentorship in the accelerator to collaboration in my latest venture. *I, Leader* is an essential read for startup founders. It masterfully merges practical insights with Tak's firsthand experiences, both from a startup and a venture capital standpoint. The book is particularly enlightening for AI entrepreneurs, showcasing Tak's profound knowledge and forward thinking in AI investment. More than a guide, this book serves as a beacon of inspiration for anyone navigating the exhilarating path of entrepreneurship.

Kyle Lu
Ex-Zeroth founder

Tak, your book describing your recent journey with starting the first accelerator in AI with brutal honesty is very inspiring. Your dedication to walk the walk making personal sacrifices to support founders in your accelerator reminds me of stories I've heard from some of the early Silicon Valley VCs. I always believe in being true to yourself and to others; life will guide you to your destiny. AI will have long-lasting effects in the tech world, just like the Internet is still evolving since 1983. Quoting from Star Wars, "May the Force be with you" in continuing your journey.

Joseph Wei
Humanitarian, conservationist, IEEE Region 6 Director-Elect 2023

An AI-focused accelerator in 2017—Tak saw it coming! Tak uncovers the precious gems that illuminate the founder's journey in launching a new company and navigating the treacherous terrain of securing initial investor funding. Drawing from extensive experience with early-stage startups, Tak imparts invaluable lessons and profound insights that outshine the knowledge of most investors. Through captivating storytelling and personal anecdotes, this book reveals the hidden gems of triumphs and tribulations experienced by founders. It is an indispensable resource for aspiring entrepreneurs and investors.

Ankit Suri

Ex-Zeroth founder, Planto founder

Tak provides valuable lessons and words of advice from his personal AI journey over the past decade. Relevant to leadership in AI, and also leadership in life - I am sure you will get something valuable out of hearing his story.

Micheael Lin

Principal, L & T Consulting Ltd.

I've known Tak for almost a decade now, and his unique way of thinking, communication style, and strategic approach have always stood out. I invite everyone to dive into" *I, Leader*", and discover invaluable wisdom shared by Tak. As we navigate the age of AI, this manifesto goes beyond a typical business book read. It guides us with a narrative of resilience, incredible foresight, and humanity, offering guidance for visionary leadership during these disruptive times.

Armin Saïdi

CEO at EZR, solving future of work challenges

With refreshing sincerity, Tak Lo has captured the often unspoken ups and downs of a modern startup founder in this collection of short, piercing reflections. A timely reminder that character, optimism through adversity, and ultimately, humanity are far from simple business clichés— they are essential to leading people in the age of AI.

Lukas Petrikas

Head of Innovation and Data Lab, Hong Kong Exchanges and Clearing Limited (HKEX)

I've known Tak since the Techstars days in London over a decade ago, and I was lucky enough to spend time with him in Hong Kong during Zeroth. His passion for supporting founders was incredible to see and work alongside in person, and I'm delighted to see he's been able to transfer that same energy and enthusiasm into this book. An essential read for anyone that wants to understand how to start, build, scale companies, accelerators, ecosystems and more.

Eamonn Carey

GP at Tera Ventures and author of *The Startup Lexicon*

Tak—as an author and as a person—has a unique take on the world that's insanely relevant as well as inspiring. His style of writing is so real: this isn't an academic lecture that will send you to sleep; it's a journey of discovery told with humility and humor. I'm not a tech person, yet the leadership lessons from Tak are as relevant for the modern manager as they are for a Silicon Valley startup. Couldn't put it down.

Alex Bowen

COO of PayMe, Hong Kong's most actively used P2P payments app

Tak's book is a game-changer, offering invaluable lessons from his own journey that resonate with anyone looking to lead in their startup and personal life. It's concise yet profound, guiding you to level up and embody the best version of yourself. A must-read for first-time founders and those eager to grow personally.

M

Founder of ShortX, a platform that allows users to profit from climate change (0xshortx on GitHub)

Riveting. The best thing since *Eat, Pray, Love.*

Brian Chien

Senior director consultant

A memory of Tak that sticks in my head: I was in HK chatting with founders at Zeroth, and the food delivery arrived. Everyone started to get food and eat, except for Tak. I asked him if he was hungry, and he said yes but he would eat when everyone else had some food… Says a lot.

Doug Scott

The UK's most active pre-seed investor

Reading this book feels like going on a journey with a true innovator, Tak, who not only dreams big but also works hard to make those dreams come true. I was captivated by the narrative woven through Tak's penned thoughts and journal snippets from years ago, filled with what feels like genuine love for manifesting new visions while making sure they are purposeful for future generations. *I, Leader* makes it clear that self-reflection and introspection are paramount for any leader in today's fast-changing world. Even when technology and AI seem to take over (who knows if or when), the human touch is still something we can't do without.

I'd recommend this book to anyone who's into technology, running a business, or leading a team, and wants to get better at what they do.

The Management Consultant

@themgmtconsult; newsletter.consultingintel.com

Much like the person I've known for years, Tak is just as generous with his humble sharings in *I, Leader*. The concise writing offers a refreshing perspective at one's startup journey, enriched by invaluable lessons that not all of us can afford to come across ourselves. I am grateful for Tak's sincerity and humility in his book, and it will no doubt inspire many founders to come.

Richard Lai

Ex-Editor-in-Chief of *Engadget Chinese*

Tak has always been on the cutting edge of technology (and sometimes the BLEEDING edge). His book *I, Leader* brings a unique perspective that combines technology and innovation with military discipline and leadership. In an ever-changing world of tech startups and AI, and volatile geopolitics, it's good to have a few nerdy soldiers around to lead the way.

Dave McClure

Founder of Practical VC, 500 Startups, and 42Geeks

If Jocko Willink had run a Tech Accelerator, that would be Tak Lo. His no-holds-barred approach to life and startup lessons is based on a rich personal history and observing the very best evolve into the biggest companies globally. Tak embodies unwavering support for founders, evident through his deep engagement in Eastern European and London startup ecosystems. I've witnessed firsthand his pivotal role in nurturing these environments, making his book a valuable resource for aspiring entrepreneurs and business leaders, distinguished by its authenticity and depth derived from his firsthand experiences as a founder and his close interactions with entrepreneurs in his portfolio.

Carlos Espinal

Managing Partner of Seedcamp and author of
the *Fundraising Field Guide*

L'eader

L,'Leader

Leadership Philosophy from the Army and Startups for the Age of AI

Tak Lo

With a foreword by **David Cohen**

To those who seek to lead in the age of AI,
lead you.

Contents

Foreword

In the foothills of the Rocky Mountains, amidst the stunning scenery of Boulder, Colorado, a remarkable journey began. It was here that a small group of entrepreneurs came together to share a vision for the future — building a community where innovation thrives, where ideas are nurtured, and where success is measured not only by financial returns but by their impact on the world.

That community was Techstars.

As one of the founders of Techstars, I've been privileged to witness the incredible evolution of our organization—from humble beginnings in a Boulder basement to a global network spanning continents and cultures. Along the way, one guiding principle remains constant, serving as the core value that guides our every decision and action: Give First.

Give First isn't just a slogan or a tagline—it's the essence of who we are as a community. It's a commitment to support one another, to share knowledge and resources, and to lift up each other. It's a philosophy that fueled the growth of Techstars from a small startup accelerator to the most active pre-seed investor in the world, empowering thousands of entrepreneurs every year.

In *I, Leader*, Tak Lo takes the spirit of Give First and applies it to the realm of leadership in the age of artificial intelligence. It's a timely exploration of the intersection between technology and humanity, between innovation and empathy. As we stand on the precipice of a new era defined by rapid technological advancement, Tak reminds us of the importance of staying grounded in our values, of remembering that true leadership is ultimately about serving others and creating a positive impact in the world.

What I find most compelling about Tak's approach is his ability to weave together insights from his own experiences as an entrepreneur and investor with broader trends shaping the future of leadership. He draws on lessons learned from Techstars' journey—from our early days in Boulder to our expansion to New York and London, where he worked—and offers practical advice and actionable strategies for navigating the challenges and opportunities that lie ahead.

As you dive into the pages of *I, Leader*, I also encourage you to embrace the ethos of Give First—to approach leadership with a spirit of generosity, and collaboration. Whether you're a seasoned executive leading a multinational corporation, or a young entrepreneur just starting out on your journey, remember that the most successful leaders are those who prioritize the needs of others, who seek to empower and uplift those around them.

In a world where technology is advancing at an exponential rate, it's easy to lose sight of what truly matters—to become so enamored with the latest products that we forget about the people behind them. But as Tak reminds us, the essence of leadership lies not in the tools we use or the strategies we employ, but in our ability to connect with and inspire others, to foster a sense of belonging that transcends boundaries.

David Cohen

Founder and CEO, Techstars

Preface

I **HAVE WAITED** all my life to write this book.

Dec 22, 2017

Go to where the action is
https://thetaklo.medium.com/
go-to-where-the-action-is-a7b7ffc78494

I have a rule to always stay close to the action. This principle has guided me from my decision to go to the military, to move to startups, and now to AI. I recently was reminded of this lesson again when we were setting up for the Beijing conference, and I told the team to stay close to the action and go to where help was most likely to be needed.

*Some of the reasons why I think this
is necessary:*

*Action is where the energy is. It is where
the things are happening the earliest
and fastest.*

*Action is hard. It's where few tread,
so there are few people or knowledge
in the field.*

*Action is leading. It creates opportuni-
ties because by definition it is where new
things are happening.*

Tom Chikoore, a Techstars founder and a mentor of mine through the Techstars Patriot Boot Camp program, met me last year when I was in Denver after skiing with my high school friends Roj Niyogi and Nick Lin. It was the first time I had seen him in years, and it was great to catch up with him after so long.

After chatting about post-Covid life and family over a beer, he said, "You were right about the AI trend."

Seven years ago, I created the world's first AI-focused accelerator. I was investing in AI before anyone else had dared to venture into the field, and in a short period of time became the most active AI investor in the world.

The accelerator was not as successful as it could have been. I had a lot of ambition, but my fund partner did not share my vision and we never managed to find a way forward together.

But I don't regret trying. I think we got many things right, such as figuring out an accelerator model for technical founders when there wasn't such a thing in Asia, and certainly not in Hong Kong.

It's amazing to see where AI is now. My recent trip to the World Economic Forum at Davos was highlighted by everyone's concern about AI, misinformation and disinformation, and how it could impact the US general election. Everyone was talking about it—royalty, heads of governments, and of course, corporates. AI has hit the mainstream.

I had known for a long time that AI would be important, but didn't think it would take off as much as it did in 2023 with Sam Altman's OpenAI. Back in 2022, the technology space was also contending with Web3 and its perversions. I like to term it "crazy cabin-fever capital" for all the stimulus money that was used to buy stupid monkey JPEGs, thinking that we would be living in a post-Zoom world and never returning to the office again. Funding was being thrown at every Web3/crypto idea or fund that came around, even if the team was anonymous.

The reversion to tech fundamentals in 2023 was refreshing—fundamentals like an actual team developing a product, what purpose the product serves, how many customers there are, and the exit path. A startup doesn't need to answer all these questions up front, but the questions can be asked, and in many cases should be.

And finally, the form in which AI came back—through an essentially consumer application—was interesting, to say the least. We had gone through the necessary but unsuccessful wave of chatbots around 2017, and that wave had thoroughly died. Sam's OpenAI was another form of chatbot, albeit with a much better engine (LLM), and it reignited everyone's imagination!

My aim with this book is simple: to showcase the leadership lessons I've learned through my trials and through my founders as I was building the world's first AI accelerator. I talk about things like values, momentum, grit, and creativity—vital concepts that I have observed in the world's best leaders, from the US Army to London Business School and the global startup world from the Valley to Beijing, referencing everything from modern finance films like *Margin Call* to timeless texts like the Taoist book *Tao Te Ching* (道德经). I also weave in my unique upbringing, having lived across the world and spent significant time in the US, Europe, and Asia, with an understanding of multiple languages and cultures.

I end the book on more practical matters: how to build an AI accelerator, and the startup scene in China.

My aim is to make it easy for founders everywhere to learn from my lessons.

I named this book, if you haven't figured it out by now, after Isaac Asimov's seminal work, *I, Robot*. The book centers on the Three Laws of Robotics:

- **The First Law:** A robot may not injure a human being or, through inaction, allow a human being to come to harm.

- **The Second Law:** A robot must obey the orders given it by human beings except where such orders would conflict with the First Law.
- **The Third Law:** A robot must protect its own existence as long as such protection does not conflict with the First or Second Law.

This reference to Asimov has come full circle, so to speak; my AI accelerator program was named after Asimov's lesser known law, Zeroth:

- **The Zeroth Law:** A robot may not injure humanity or, through inaction, allow humanity to come to harm.

The name fits perfectly because the aim of my program was to accelerate the development of AI leaders toward the benefit of humanity.

AI is the Future

I'M A MAN who has to work. Has to output. But for the two years before 2016, I hadn't created anything. I was biding my time, trying to find something worthy of my precious energy.

I found it in early 2016.

I had left London in 2014, after finishing my tenure helping start Techstars London with Jon Bradford and Jess Williamson. I knew what I was good at (accelerators), and had been searching for a fund thesis worthy of my accelerator expertise and a long-term commitment to building a startup ecosystem.

General technology funds were not a fit for me, as I did not see the competitive advantage of starting yet another accelerator in another crowded market

(China). Further, I had become frustrated with general technology—akin to the quote, "We asked for flying cars, and all we got was 140 characters." I was quickly falling out of love with tech marketing about raising (both from VCs and startups) and the prospect of yet another startup that made marginal improvements in life. I wanted to back startups and founders that wanted to make a significant, not minuscule, impact on the way we lived.

At the same time, there was something emerging in London that I felt was not being served globally, and for which I could carve out a leadership role. At that point, Azeem Azhar was focused on AI and its impact on humanity, creating a content empire called Exponential View. Jaan Tallinn from Skype was pondering the ethics of AI as he established the Center for Existential Risk.

I saw the future—plain as day.

To me, artificial intelligence was alluring in that it took technological concepts to their philosophical extreme, impacting human nature, nay, even human civilization. It asked fundamental questions of ourselves about what it meant to be human, and hinted at the boundaries between machine and human. It begged answers, none of which were available as our limited cognition failed to grasp the possibilities. It prompted questions such as *What is reality? What is creativity?* and *What purpose do we serve as a species?*

It melded philosophy and technology, Descartes and Demis. It felt worthy of my time and attention.

I made the leap.

I quickly gathered a pitch deck, investors, and mentors. I knew the accelerator process and the formula on how to run a successful program, since I had been trained by the very best. My LPs backed me. I hired the team.

On July 5, 2016, I wrote a blog post that birthed a new concept.

The Singular Reason Why I'm Starting Zeroth

*https://thetaklo.medium.com/
the-singular-reason-why-im-starting-zeroth-9af4dc39bdb4*

It's currently 12:23 AM in Da Nang, Vietnam. I'm in the hotel lobby by myself, finishing this post, just having had a drinks conversa-

tion about Brexit, American politics, and third/fourth/fifth culture people. And despite a full day traveling with family and working, I'm still energized.

Energized by a singular focus. Because as of July 1, 2016, I created Zeroth.ai, an early-stage funding program focused on developing Asian Artificial Intelligence and Machine Learning startups. We will be taking our initial cohort of startups starting in November, for 3 months.

There are many reasons why Zeroth exists. I have a deep rooted belief that AI will indeed change the world as we know it in the next 5–10 years. I believe that there is serious technical and entrepreneurial talent in Asia that's waiting to create a world-beating AI company. I believe in contributing the knowledge and network I have accumulated to benefit an ecosystem I live in—Hong Kong, because it's so behind in tech.

But if I had to distill the reasons to a singular belief (for that's a true testament of the real, true reason)—I created Zeroth because

I believe in leading. I want to lead increasingly rapid innovation in Asia. I want to lead backing early stage founders in a very conservative culture. I want to lead the charge that the Asian tech ecosystem can be stronger, together.

If you are a founder or know a founder with the same singular belief, I would love to hear it. My new email is tak@zeroth.ai.

Let's build Zeroth together.

There was no going back.

The Return to Innocence

I LAUNCHED MY very first startup back in college—if you don't count selling porn in high school on 3.5-inch floppy disks.

It was with my high school friend Roj Niyogi, who was a far more brilliant entrepreneur than I but somehow pushed me to become the CEO of the business, a reverse-auction for OEM parts called ElectricOne. Think of it like Alibaba, ten years early.

But we were so naive. We knew nothing about OEM parts, far less about reverse-auctions, and much, much less about building a business. We were only 22.

I couldn't lead the startup. I didn't know what direction we should take, I didn't know business strategy, and I'd never managed accounts for any enterprise.

But Roj believed in me as a leader. And the more I thought about it, it wasn't the tactical things I knew or didn't. It was my belief in myself as a leader that I lacked.

I needed to develop the courage to lead.

So I joined the military. To be specific, I joined the United States Army, the oldest military organization in the country, as an enlisted member. Normally, recruits such as I with college degrees would become officers, obtaining prestige and a higher pay grade. But because I was not a US citizen at that point, I could only get in as a grunt, a working man.

I didn't mind. I went in to learn how to lead, and it didn't matter from where.

I graduated top ten in my boot camp company, despite having never shot a rifle in my life before. I graduated from the Air Assault Course, "the toughest ten days in the Army," and was honorably discharged for serving with high standards of conduct and discipline during my commitment.

Most importantly, I learned what makes good leaders, great leaders, and shit leaders.

Sergeant Willy was a man's man, his well-leathered face covered in pockmarks the size of the Chesapeake Bay crater. When you spoke to Sergeant Willy, he didn't reply; he growled back. And even when he growled, he didn't say but a few words at a time. He always had a cigarette cloud surrounding him, so you never really quite saw his face behind the cover of gray.

But Sergeant Willy was someone you could be in the foxhole with. You knew you had his loyalty and he had yours. He couldn't do everything, but he did the right things right. He would lead the charge into fire, first to fight, when others would cower.

Sergeant Willy helped me learn the difference between leaders.

I left the military and joined a defense consulting firm and business school. But I still had the itch to do a startup, and I was better equipped to lead.

I joined my second startup after graduating from London Business School, a business called The Travelst. It was a travel content business—think travel meets Gilt Groupe—and we would sell affiliate links on travel and travel-related goods.

It was with this business that I went to the Techstars Patriot Boot Camp program, a mini accelerator for military veterans, almost as a last chance to get funding and direction on where we needed to go. There I met Tom Chikoore, Boot Camp founder Taylor McLemore, and the CEO of Techstars, David Cohen. And through that last Hail Mary is how The Travelst ended up not entering Techstars (once they learned more about the business and realized it wasn't a fit!) but instead how I got a job with the organization.

I worked first in the New York Office under Nicole Glaros (one of Techstars' first employees), and then with Jon Bradford and Jess Williamson building Techstars London, the first international program and first in Europe. When I left, we had grown to five programs alone in Europe, and I was the most senior director, having worked with three startup cohorts.

Despite my experience, I would not say I'm the best startup leader. I've probably failed so many times that I often think I have imposter syndrome.

To compound that, I have also seen my fair share of founder failings. Like corpses on the battlefield, each story drags me down as I weigh what could I have done differently to help.

What I mean is that when I invest, I invest in the people, their journeys, their struggles, and hopefully, their triumphs. Of course, I want everyone to succeed, but that's not the game we play; there will always be a fair share of losses. Those losses, and how the founders go through those losses, really do impact me, as much as I don't show it. And to some degree I can't show it because I have to stay strong, to be there for them.

No one knows the extent to which I cared for my founders. I would call my founders and ask how they were doing emotionally, even when my investment in the startup was in real danger of going to flames. I extended a helping hand from my personal funds when theirs were low. I even rented my own personal property for free so that one of my founders could have a place to live.

I did my very best, but my best still failed my founders sometimes.

One of the things I have learned is to keep going forward. When my fund partner made it almost impossible for me to go on, I left Zeroth with my team. I had abandoned ship, using a Navy example, on my founders and LPs, those who had chosen me to go forward on that path. But did I have a greater obligation to the LPs, to go down with the ship?

This was the difficult question I faced on a boat with two captains.

Thus, as much as I'm burdened by these struggles and failures, I must go on. I must keep moving forward to learn, tell these stories of founders' lessons, and teach the next founders and generations of entrepreneurs. That's my responsibility and gift to the world.

They Become Your Destiny

Values are where everything starts. You start from this core, and how you behave and conduct yourself is just a derivative of those values. So it's really important to be clear on your values: what you stand for, and what you accept and what you do not.

Enter Marko Srsan. I first met Marko at a Seedcamp event in Croatia, where he was a marketing hustler in love with the European startup ecosystem. He approached me with this overwhelming puppy-dog enthusiasm, and I, in my usual reserved way, deflected that excited energy. I would think he thought I was a proper dick.

It turns out our meeting was fortuitous, because pretty quickly we started looking for Hackstars, or business interns, for our upcoming inaugural Techstars London cohort. I had a conversation with him, and of course he expressed his overwhelming interest in joining us. But then I had the gall to reject him.

I immediately regretted it. Here was a young man who had passionately contributed to the ecosystem entirely as a volunteer, who had had the courage to approach me and offer to help out more, and the desire to move to London and take a leap of faith in our inaugural program. He had all the qualities of an entrepreneur—and I had missed this!

I went back to him and asked whether he would like to join my program. He did and became a superb program manager.

November 30, 2016

10 Values

I spend a lot of time looking back and figuring out how to communicate and distill my learnings to benefit others. I had written a similar blog post when I passed on my Techstars post to Marko, the current PM, based on my blog post, How To Best Serve Startups.

The below are some of my values based on what I've seen and learned, to be passed to Z01 and the Zeroth team:

Discipline and focus in thought and action.

Force yourself into the rhythm of deciding quickly.

Obtain clarity through action.

1 action is better than >1.

Execute with pace and precision.

Embrace that the conflict of ideas is good because the best ideas win.

Each individual is accountable absolutely.

Make yourself and your team successful and everything else falls in line.

Recognize what 1 thing drives 90% of the results.

Build a company so that it can exist without you.

It was from a spirit of deep love for my program and what we'd built that I'd entrusted it to Marko, to continue the work of serving the London entrepreneurial community. Those values resonated with me as I handed things over to him, and from what I remember, this was the very last blog post I wrote during my tenure.

I think I had a tear in my eye when I wrote it. That's how much it meant to me.

The values in this post are the core distillation of the lessons I learned from the military. Team first. Build things better than when you inherited them. Personal accountability. Speed. Focus. Discipline.

But the most important value of all of them? It's embedded in the title of the other blog post referenced in the "10 Values" post, "How to Best Serve Startups."

To serve. To put yourself last. To put the mission before you. To put yourself at the mercy of whatever magnificent power there is, and to paraphrase the words of Indiana Jones in *Indiana Jones and the Last Crusade*, "be the penitent man who kneels before God."

Those values and service orientation are how I started Zeroth. I wanted to have those qualities embodied in everything I did, in Zeroth, and in the team culture. I knew how much those qualities had added to the London ecosystem, and I wanted the same DNA in what we were creating from scratch.

Insane in the Membrane

Mentor madness. It means subjecting a startup founder to the maximum amount of feedback in the shortest amount of time.

It was an internal term at Techstars, and something we used at Zeroth as well.

Mentor madness means in practical terms that founders meet with eight or ten mentors, ranging from VCs to angels to product people, back to back for 30-minute quick-burst meetings, for one entire day. If you ask any Techstars or Zeroth founder, it's the most mentally exhausting period in the program.

But despite the mental burden, this method is a super-powerful tool. One, it engages the startup and broader business community in a meaningful way. Corporates, service providers, later stage startup founders, and other members of the community are giving advice to the founder, with no expectation of any return other than to help. This places the entrepreneur at the forefront of importance, and orients the ecosystem in the right way.

Two, it gives the founder loads of third party advice, much more than they normally could get or figure out on their own. And because the advice is comprehensive, from all angles, the entrepreneur is able to discover potential issues they had not yet contemplated.

Because of this intense mentor madness experience, I have a unique framework for startup leaders on how to process feedback at scale, which every founder faces—there's always someone willing to give their two cents on how to run their business.

November 14, 2016

How To Process Feedback

Feedback is complex because it comes in different forms and irregularly. Different feedback has different themes (product, process, etc.) and timing (now, later, etc.). Feedback is also biased based on the giver's world view, and sometimes what he or she says is indicative, not prescriptive.

Feedback is complex because it's hard to process the above and weigh the feedback accurately. Do you weigh the feedback that is timely more than feedback that isn't? Do you weigh feedback from experts more than those from non-experts?

I think of processing feedback first as a classification problem. I classify feedback based on certain themes (product, process, team, strategy, or fundraising). They may even be in an 'other' category that is outside of my world-view, but could be important. Classifying feedback first allows me to try to figure out what the giver is really saying, not what they just said. I also try to disregard who said the feedback and classify feedback based on the insight, not the giver.

I then weigh that feedback based on the giver. Every giver has bias, whether he or she knows it or not. The good feedback givers state up-front what biases they may have, the normal ones don't, and the worst ones intentionally push their feedback despite their biases. The two biases that may show up are geographic and stage bias. Usually certain feedback can pertain well to certain geographies and stages in startups.

One way to weigh feedback is to say, based on all the feedback received, what are the 1 or 2 that you resonate with? I realize that this is an imperfect way to determine weight, but the bottom-up method of weighting (assigning percentages) is oftentimes inefficient and subject to the same biases that a top-down method will have anyways. When bias is the same, go for the method that is more time-efficient.

Classifying feedback is still the most important thing. What exactly is the feedback? What category does it belong to?

But most importantly, *what are they really saying?*

There are many ways to explain, for example, that your product isn't resonating with the user. So it's your job as the leader to drill down and try to get a handle on the issue. Is it a delivery issue? A user interface issue? A competitiveness issue?

Sometimes what it takes is asking more questions. Sometimes it's giving your customers different offerings until you have evidence that something is working, without direct feedback.

What matters is getting to the core—what they are really saying.

∞

Another key component of separating the signal from the noise is to focus on the right things. A founder's life has many distractions—fundraising, events, team meetings, customer interactions, speaking engagements, the list goes on and on.

A founder needs to be able to identify what exactly to focus on, and be absolutely ruthless in executing it.

November 14, 2016

The Two Components of Focus

Focus has two components—one is the identification of what to focus on, and the other is the habit of executing focus. Each part reinforces the other—without identification, habit is applied in the wrong way and is wasted energy. Without habit and discipline, identification is merely a theoretical thought exercise.

Identification is a product of disciplined thinking. Identification is sitting down every day and devoting some mental energy to what should be focused on. Like an artist that creates a statue from carving a little bit everyday from a large rock, identification is carving out slightly more every day to identify the very essence.

There are shortcuts to identification. One way is to source outside inputs and to get a sense of what other things to focus on. Another way is to bounce ideas off other people, to get their inputs. But there is no substitute to digesting those inputs, channeling back into your thinking, and carving out a bit more every day.

Habit is a product of disciplined doing. Habit is sitting down every day and devoting some physical energy to doing the same exact thing. There is no substitute to getting a butt in a seat or the body somewhere, every day, and going through the routine day in and day out.

Unlike identification, there are no shortcuts to developing habits. Habits are developed through sheer willpower; when others are partying, you ignore it and stay in to work. When others are watching the Cubs win the World Series, you shut off the TV and build. When others say you're a party pooper, you say yes I am and you focus on the bigger goal. When others say you're weird, you say yes and you go back to building.

We had a saying at Techstars and Zeroth that the best startups would be in the room until the wee hours of the night. They would spend daylight on working and gathering feedback, and then spent the night iterating and building.

This was especially impressive in accelerators held in big cities. Techstars in London and Zeroth in Hong Kong are usually party to loads of startup events in the evenings. What we found is that the strong startups would attend these events in order to network and get customer feedback, then head back to the office to work.

And I enjoyed being in the office with these startups at night.

When I was building Zeroth, I would blog daily on taklo.co. The blog was my daily practice of identifying something to focus on (distilling one key lesson from the busy-ness of the day), and executing on it (blogging).

Through that disciplined action of blogging, I picked up the ability to discern very quickly the core of any one thing I wanted to write about. In blogging, I learned you can start from the end goal of wanting to explain that key thing. And like solving a maze, you could work backward from that end goal and figure out the most efficient and clear path to the beginning.

That path to finding that end goal, that one thing you want to focus on, is a key skill not only in blogging, but in trying to unpack the craziness of each and every day to learn something new. It is through that process that founders can get 1 percent better every day.

November 10, 2016

The One Thing

What is the one thing you've learned today?

What is the one thing you've extrapolated from all the conversations you'd had?

What is the one thing that sticks out at you and makes you wonder, Why didn't I think of that?

What is the one thing that the same time tomorrow, you'll remember today? What is the one thing, not number two or three?

> *What is the one thing that you will action—right now?*
>
> *What is the one thing you've learned today?*

When you filter your day through the tight lens of one of these questions, you end the day focused on one thing. That one thing could be actionable, it could be philosophical, it could be educational.

But that one thing is what separates just another day from a day that is focused on learning. And that learning, when compounded, is what makes growth happen.

∞

At Techstars and at Zeroth, we ended the three-month program with a Demo Day where the startup founders present themselves and their company on stage. And when I say stage, it really was! The largest demo day I've organized was at Techstars London, where we sat over 600 people at the Genesis Cinema in East London.

When presenting at a Demo Day, founders have to learn to deal with pressure and not to lose control of themselves in the hoopla of the moment. Similarly, in startup life, there are a lot of external forces, like fundraising with investors or closing a deal with a corporate partner. That term sheet may be pulled at the last moment by the investor, or the corporate partner may decide to go with a competitor when you need that contract the most. There are many opportunities to go insane.

The best way to stay sane is to stay in the moment.

February 24, 2017

Today

It's a big day. You've hustled for 3 months and built something from nothing. You've argued and fought. You've embraced tough feedback and asked for more. You've stretched beyond your comfort zone. You are proving to yourself that you can handle this.

It's also not a big day. In the spectrum of the days in a year, in 10, or in a lifetime. It's composed of 24 hours just like any other day, of the natural sunlight and sunset. It contains events that are quite normal in a startup's life, like pitching and talking to investors.

Both ideas are correct, despite being opposites. For me, to reconcile both means to fully embrace today. To feel energized when I look backward and see how much has been accomplished, and to be rational when I look forward to seeing the future ahead. And to balance both time horizons in my head means to be in the moment, enjoy it, and to live it completely.

Feb 22, 2017

Concentration at the Final Moment

It's easy to lose focus at the very end of a process. The mind thinks about the next stage and the next process, and naturally loses grip on the current situation. The mind can't wait until this current process is over.

But actually, this is the point where it is most critical for success or failure. People's perception of success or failure is defined by the last thing they see or experience. All the previous work is considered a sunk cost. Fairly or unfairly, that final moment is what defines a process.

During the run-up to this moment, it's critical to focus on the process even more extremely. Focusing on the process slows down the perception of time and allows for better focus on individual process components. It allows for better distraction management by not focusing on the things outside the process. It ultimately helps concentration and the performance of the final moment.

I believe a lot in the importance of focus. There are so many distractions out there, so many opinions on how to build a startup, so many pieces of funding news that make you feel as if you suck and are the worst CEO on Hacker News.

Everyone runs their own race, in their own time. The moment you stop running your own race in your own way, you lose. Run the race, but to your tempo.

Because once you know your tempo, you become free. Free to be in the moment. Free to make choices. Free to be you. And the universe will reward you for being you.

December 21, 2016

Be Free

Connor McGregor, the UFC fighter, says that when he is in the Octagon about to fight, he is "free." I love that word and I think I know that feeling.

Being free means being only in the moment. It means you let external events ebb and flow. You react according to those events— sometimes you are passive and let the action dictate movement. Sometimes you are aggressive and dictate the action. You don't think about the past, and you don't think about the future. You are free of fear, anger, happiness, and any other emotion.

You are in the now; you are now, now is you.

Turn! Turn! Turn! (To Everything There Is A Season)

IN THE UNITED States Navy, there's a saying called "Win the transitions." It's when a submarine surfaces from the deep sea that it is most at risk. In the same vein, I believe founders need to get a sense of when transitions happen so that they can plan their attack accordingly.

The very nature of startups is change. One moment you could be learning how to fundraise, the next about quantum computing and how it impacts your business. One moment your startup could be worth $11 billion and you're on the cover of *The*

Information, and the next you're getting calls from concerned investors on your company policies.

A founder must understand change, when it happens, and what to do. Like a piece of music you've never heard before, you can learn to recognize and anticipate tempo changes.

I learned this during my first winter at Techstars London, when I was trying to meet with founders to let them know of the upcoming program. I was furiously recruiting as this was my first program, eager to make an impression and build the best cohort I could. I knew that this first cohort would make or break our reputation in London and in Europe as a whole.

No one could be found.

Instead, everybody was skiing in Zermatt or in Germany at the Christmas markets. No matter how many emails I sent or cold calls I made, no one responded to emails or was available for coffee. Europe had shut down for the winter.

So I ditched all my efforts and binged on *Breaking Bad*. There was no point in aggravating and winding myself up when I couldn't do anything about it.

Similarly, when it comes to change, a startup founder needs to recognize momentum, when there is movement and action driving toward something. Momentum is one of those things, like porn, that you know when you see it, but it's hard to describe.

Porn and momentum. Never thought I would draw a link between those two things.

December 14, 2016

Momentum

Momentum is what happens when things or events start happening in a way that is favorable to a company or person. There is a distinct feeling between pre-momentum (things were so damn hard!) and post-momentum (things are so much easier!).

The difference between pre-and post-momentum is simply that external startup forces are more aligned to what you are doing. Sometimes it's because you shifted the market segment you're targeting, or the market timing is much better now, or you're much better at pitching what you're doing. All those factors and more can be reasons.

When post-momentum happens, it seems important to keep riding and even accelerate. No one knows how long post-momentum will last, so the logical thing to do in an undefined time period is to continue or increase the velocity. If there is insufficient time, labor, or other resources to capitalize on post-momentum, the logical answer seems to be to hire or find more resources, because that is solvable whereas momentum is not.

Pre-momentum and post-momentum rely on the same fundamental internal work ethic and tempo. That tempo remains fairly constant over time. That tempo is the bedrock, despite what external things happen.

Internal tempo is also important because momentum can disappear. Post-momentum can morph back into pre-momentum, the good times can change to the bad. When that happens, the tempo is the one constant

*to ride out fluctuating times before the next
wave appears.*

*It's important to get to this place in the critical
points in life. Those moments will define how
your life unfolds, and to be totally free in
those moments largely dictates the trajectory
in which you go.*

During the zero interest rate policy (ZIRP) cycle of much of the 2010s and early 2020s, things were largely good for startups. If you had a good idea, a network, and traction, your startup would probably have gotten funded. If you were lucky to have created a startup then, it was a good time.

Now, in the post-ZIRP world, things are hard. Valuations are low. Investors have more bargaining power.

In essence, fundraising momentum has slowed. But know that times will be better. Stay low, bide your time, find a sustainable model, and prepare to fundraise when times are better.

∞

Many founders believe that they always have to be on the offense, to be active all the time. But to leverage momentum sometimes means being patient and waiting for the situation to develop.

I'm not advocating for a founder to be passive; what I am suggesting is to be actively patient, waiting with a plan for the right time to execute.

It's like in *Braveheart*, when Mel Gibson commands the front line to hold. Then hold some more. And when they don't think they can hold anymore, they hold just a bit more. The enemy gets so close, so over-extended, that they can't retreat anymore.

It's similar to the tai chi fighting principle "Lead them to emptiness." They push and you resist, just enough that they keep pushing, but not too much that they're on the defensive. While resisting just enough, you guide them further and further away from their core, from their solid ground.

Then you attack.

Jan 12, 2017

Waiting for The Situation to Develop

There are times when the best course of action is to wait. As an entrepreneur I'm primed to move and accomplish, but that isn't always the best move given an array of moves.

Sometimes that happens because there is no additional information that could be gained by moving. By pinging the customer again for the umpteenth time with no significant reason or update, you gain no information from the interaction. You might as well have done nothing than waste time on an update.

Or that moving would be a marginal increase in risk. What if instead of pinging that customer you go directly to her boss? That can have significant downsides to the entire process.

Or that another unit of effort would be more productive somewhere else. Some would call

> *this momentum, where instead of fighting against the wave you go the direction where there is least friction. That is a prudent move, because sometimes momentum in a different area produces momentum in your desired area, in a roundabout way.*

Leaders are primed to move and to act.

But don't confuse activity with movement. You can be active without moving. You can be a leopard, ready to pounce, muscles and sinews relaxed and ready to load. But not moving.

Until the right moment.

∞

By thinking about change and momentum first, you change the priority to understanding the process. You don't think about the goal—about being first, for example—but about understanding change and timing, and harnessing the momentum. Like a good sailor, you learn to read the current and the wind, and to harness both to your advantage.

Once you let go of the goal and understand the nature of change, you are truly free to pursue being first or best, but not shackled by the pursuit.

October 19, 2016

Being First or Best

Being first is a common badge of honor. The title means that you were a visionary, that you saw what was coming earlier than the herd. In that sense, being first is saying that you're much better than average. Way better in fact.

But being visionary does not equate to being successful. Seeing something early and acting on being early are two different stories. I could say all day "I thought about Facebook BEFORE Facebook," but the fact is that someone else named Mark thought about it, and executed it. In that sense, being visionary is a mere platitude, because of course someone had thought about some idea at some point.

Being first is "leading thinking." One says "first" to establish the lead in others' minds. It is merely a thought exercise to establish brand presence.

Being best is also another common badge of honor. The phrase also serves to remind others that one is different from the herd, better than average. However, the difference is that being best conveys an execution element, in that you did something to become better than average.

Being best is "laggard thinking." One says "best" after one compares to the rest of the population and sees a brand presence to be exploited.

The best or the first don't usually think this way, however. They usually think of those titles not as thresholds to get to, but as a continuous process toward that never-ending goal. Athletes care about being the best or first, but they care more about being better every single day to get to that. And they do it day in and day out, without fail.

> *It's not that the best or first don't care about those titles. It's more because they know that being best or first can come and go. All they care about is maximizing the best they can be, i.e., the process, and the results will speak for themselves.*

Don't obsess about titles and status about being first or best, because that can change. Care about the process, and be patient with the process. And one day—that patience will be rewarded.

As former UK prime minister Benjamin Disraeli once said, "Patience is a necessary ingredient of genius."

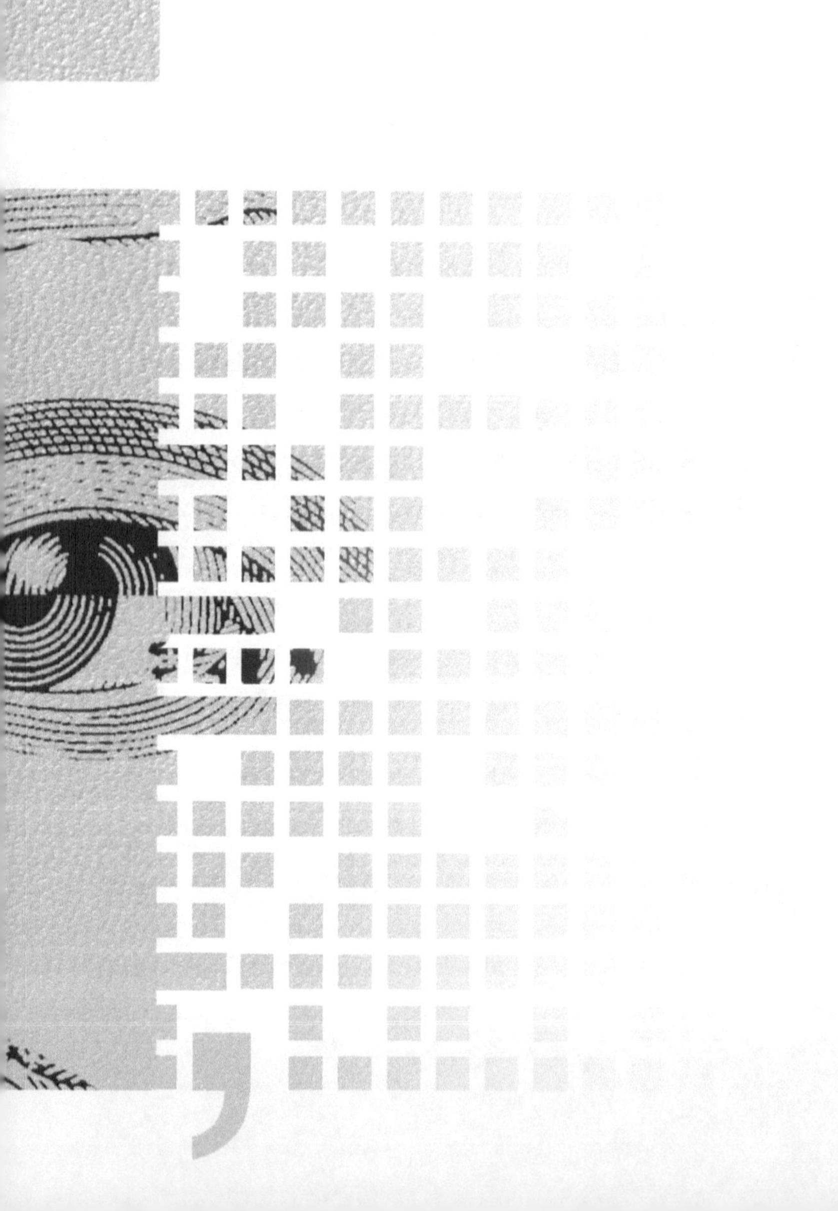

We Didn't Start the Fire

STORYTELLING IS SUCH a key skill for a founder.

I don't fancy myself a natural storyteller. It's taken me years of writing blogs, LinkedIn posts, Tweets, and even Instagram to confidently say I think I even have a grasp on telling a story.

But as a startup leader, it's important to tell a great story of the mission of the company and its people, to inspire outsiders and the team on the company's direction, its purpose, its North Star.

The most common way a startup leader tells a story is through its investor pitch. But most pitching advice from investors misses its mark by not talking about emotional resonance.

A pitch, in its most direct form, is really quite simple: problem, solution/product, traction, market size, and team.

But a pitch with emotional timbre is able to weave all those distinctive elements into a cohesive whole, making it much more likely to resonate with the listener.

Feb 15, 2017

My Secret to a Good Presentation

Is to communicate something where every concept I say has an emotional component to it. Some parts of it may invoke anger and aggression, some pride of what we created from scratch, some incredulity at doing something no one has done. There are some presentations where I almost cried because of the depth of emotions.

I take each presentation as my very last and try to put it all on the stage. It can be a tiring process but I think an audience can feel authentic emotions. I take this approach from observing great singers. When you see Adele on stage, there's a connection you feel because you know she's singing exactly what she's feeling at the moment with the lyrics. She leaves it on the stage, holding nothing back, being in the moment.

If I can drop the mic after my presentation and say "Tak Lo out," I know I did everything I could.

Emotional resonance is key. Maybe you're jaded and think you don't need to show emotion when you're pitching to an investor.

But think about it from the other side. You have investors getting pitched all day long. If a pitch is mechanical and doesn't emotionally resonate, they will forget it.

A good pitch needs to take something from you, a bit of your soul, a bit of your emotion. You need to sacrifice that emotion and gift it to the pitch. Rest assured, the listener will receive and resonate with your gift.

∞

Getting to a great story or pitch is rarely a matter of adding content. Oftentimes, it's a matter of subtraction. People make the mistake of adding, when they should be subtracting.

Adding covers up, while subtracting gets to the core. Which one do you think people want to see?

Feb 21, 2017

A Good Story

A good story has a single theme centered around it; it has one central concept that is said repeatedly and consistently.

A good story is like a good song; it has a beginning, a middle, and an end. The parts have an internal logic that works throughout it and binds the entire thing together.

A good story is like ceramics, where you take a lump of clay and gradually reduce and shape the excess to get to the core.

> *A good story is a process of deconstructing why something matters and what the one point truly is. Asking constantly why is a good way to deconstruct.*
>
> *A good story stands on its own in that it is complete with the one point it tries to make. It doesn't require any other points.*
>
> *A good story teaches something new or introduces a new concept to the world. It opens the mind to a new possibility or teaching that was previously unconsidered.*

This blog post was also inspired by one of my favorite quotes in the Tao Te Ching (道德经):

> *Thirty spokes share the hub of a wheel;*
> *yet it is its center that makes it useful.*
> *You can mold clay into a vessel;*
> *yet, it is its emptiness that makes it useful.*
> *Cut doors and windows from the walls of a house;*
> *but the ultimate use of the house*
> *will depend on that part where nothing exists.*
> *Therefore, something is shaped into what is;*

but its usefulness comes from what is not.

We often mistake more for better. More words. More social media. More explanation.

No—better is better. And to get better, you often have to reduce your pitch to its core, its essence.

And through that process of reduction, everything becomes clearer.

∞

One of the most impressive pitches I've ever seen was by Giorgio Patrini from Sensity, whose company could detect deepfakes, ultra-realistic computer-generated videos.

His pitch would start with three videos, of an older-aged woman with her silver hair turning in the wind as she was strolling in the open fields, or a young innocent toddler taking his first steps through the park with his parents. They were videos you might see advertised by GoPro to document key moments in life.

Then he would casually remark that all those videos were fake and AI generated. They were not real people, in real situations, in real life.

The investors' mouths would drop to the floor.

He had literally made the unreal real.

Feb 14, 2017

How to Make the Unreal Real

There's a few ways I see to make imaginary things seem like real things.

Start rooting the unreal to something insanely real. Magicians do this first by drawing attention to a deck of cards, which is insanely normal and something everyone can relate to. A deck of cards should, in almost all circumstances, obey laws of normal physics and logic.

Draw people to the very personal way you see the world. Sometimes what you are describing is a very far-out future of the world, and what you need is to describe how

> *you think about that world and how you came to it. If the audience understands where you come from, the logic is that they will believe where you want to go.*

Drawing people to your worldview is what gets them looking through your lens. So be personal. Explain each and every aspect of how you look at the world. Spare no details.

By being transparent, you become the real you. And others will love you for that.

∞

One of my favorite lessons about storytelling is from a visit to Masayoshi Son, the founder of the famous Japanese firm Softbank, when my team and I were invited there to pitch right before Christmas in 2015.

I remember receiving that email—it was right around the time Softbank launched its mega VC fund Vision Fund—and I was very excited to have the opportunity to meet with the visionary himself.

I immediately booked the next flight I could to Tokyo to meet him.

I remember strolling into Softbank's office, and downstairs was Travis Kalanick from Uber talking to a group of Japanese people. I presumed Masa himself was within that group, probably about to jet off to a sushi restaurant to close the investment. Masa likely wouldn't be at my meeting, I thought. And he wasn't.

The meeting was good but inconclusive in terms of investment, at least through Masa's fund. But I remember his team's last words as we departed.

Jan 21, 2016

100x Your Thinking

I used to think that 10x thinking was breaking the system. Recently, I was introduced to 100x, and that breaks even my mind on how far to reach forward.

If 2x thinking doesn't stress the system, then 10x does break it and begs for a new system, and 100x is creating an entirely new system that may or may not have elements of the old, but definitely incorporates learnings from the old. 100x impacts the way we think about every element.

But 100x thinking also requires honing in on which elements make the biggest impact. Elements that make little or no impact should be discarded, so the key elements make all the impact. And in this case, the key elements should drive a majority of the 100x needed.

100x thinking also puts you in the rarefied community of people who think about long-term problems and needle-moving actions. That's something special.

It blew me away when I first heard that. It almost made up for the fact I didn't get to meet Masa himself.

Surrender, Not Control

LEADERS AREN'T NECESSARY for an organization just because they can execute; at a later stage, somebody else usually takes over the execution role. A leader needs to be creative and think about the world differently. To chart an untrodden path to go forward.

A CEO should be mindfully present in the future. They need to be able to set the course on where the company should go, or in Wayne Gretsky's words, "to skate to where the puck is going."

Jan 5, 2017

Time Travel

Michel Cassius, friend but more like mentor, fellow angel investor, and CEO of Bookatable and I talked about this concept about how to live in the future.

As a CEO, it's important to imagine what 20, 30, maybe 300 years beyond looks like, for the sake of the company. He suggests thinking about that future, and working backward from there. The key is to be extremely concrete when working backward—how things will actually change around all of us, based on that supposed future.

We talked a bit about how often he does it, and it really depends on the CEO and the nature of the business. I suppose it's a function of how fast-moving the industry or business is. It's also basically the equivalent of annual planning, but much more timely and regular.

> *I usually learn something new from Michel*
> *every time I talk to him. He's a combination*
> *of someone who has tactically done things,*
> *put things together in a coherent philosophy,*
> *and has the patience to teach those lessons*
> *to a young person like me. Everyone should*
> *have one of those.*

I like what Jeremy Irons' character says about his role as CEO in *Margin Call*: "I'm here for one reason, and one reason alone. I'm here to guess what the music might do a week, a month, a year from now. That's it. Nothing more."

∞

"How can one become more creative?" I can see founders asking. Well, as my kids' last headmaster at Malvern College, Dr. Robin Lister says, it's okay to be bored. In fact, the school insists that the kids be bored a lot of the time.

Being Bored

Work in modern society places a premium on executing, being busy, and increasing the volume of getting things done. Although production has a role in the modern work schedule, the opposite of production has to have a role as well. This opposite is no production, or simply, being bored.

Being bored is the act of allocating some time everyday to the act of no production. It is the act of focusing on the opposite of outputs, on focusing on inputs. It is the act of suspending the monkey brain and focusing on sensory input in different forms, whether it be through art, music, sports, or a good meal.

Being bored works on the creative side of the brain. It allows new inputs to reflect, change, and morph previous ideas. It allows deeper reflection and insights to be gained from time.

Being bored is not non-work. It's work in a different degree, in building up the

> *underlying logic and connections between disparate ideas. Being bored is still work, just not as obvious.*
>
> *Being bored is valuing the long-term. Short-term work produces output and results, but long-term produces structures that drive impact. Being bored says that you care about the long-term, at the expense of the short-term.*

Being bored means surrendering to the whims of the day, of a group, or to a greater power. It means not having an agenda or control of the situation. It's total surrender, which is why it is so hard to do.

In this day and age, it is hard to be bored. There is a prestige element; by being busy or invited to special events, you are perceived to be important. There is a FOMO element, where social media makes things appear fun or exciting.

But how many of those things do you really enjoy? Do you really have to go? Or are you going just to take an Instagram picture?

Resist the urge to be busy. Be bored. Being bored is good.

∞

To be creative, sometimes you have to find creative role models. Then, like an actor utilizing method acting, you have to role-play being creative in order to become creative.

So go out there and find a creative visionary you admire, and try to think through their motivations and become them.

December 12, 2016

Visionaries

Some people are known to be visionaries. People like Freddie Mercury, David Bowie, Prince, Lady Gaga, Michael Jackson, and Elon Musk aren't known to be just like everyone else. Their way of being, of communicating and representing themselves seem to be at odds with the rest of society.

Those visionaries aren't different because they want to be—it's because they are different.

> *The different way these visionaries dress and communicate is a function of their authentic differences, not the other way around. I think that's the definition of a true visionary.*
>
> *Part of the difference of being a visionary, I believe, is an ability to embody a craft into a visionary's being. If you hear the stories of Freddie Mercury and Prince, you hear the legendary work ethic and devotion to music and sound. Their ability to make music is a function of their constant devotion to their craft and making their craft a core part of their being.*
>
> *Being a visionary is to take a craft and live in its future. And to push yourself further and further into that future. To surround yourself with other visionaries of a craft and push each other forward. To mentally be in that space for as long as possible, every day.*

I've always admired Richard Branson, Jay Z, and Lady Gaga. Who do you admire and want to be?

∞

Where you are also influences your creative potential. Sometimes breaking up your location can unlock creativity.

That's why writers like Hemingway loved to travel. When you shift your location, that physical change jolts your body and mind to look at things differently. Layer on the shift in culture and language, and your mind truly does shift its perspective.

I find myself being extremely creative when I'm traveling on a plane or a train, like my recent trip to Davos. There's something about being 38,000 feet in the air or on a train with limited internet access, little distractions, and a bit of wine that lets my mind wander.

September 25, 2016

How I Learned to be Creative

I just spent the weekend in Seoul. I try not to do that so that I get to see my family over the weekend, but the timing of trips meant that I had to spend one weekend away.

I was relatively bored on Sunday, so I went to a local cafe and enjoyed the weather and some wine. I brought some pen and paper, which I use a ton more for brainstorming. And then the creativity hit me.

I furiously started to write. I filled up nearly all my free pages. I started to think in different directions and the possibilities of things. My mind was literally freed up.

I learned a lesson: having a fixed location is not absolutely necessary, but it creates an atmosphere of comfort where the physical needs are satisfied so the mind can explore. Being bored is absolutely necessary because it creates an empty space for the mind to wander. And usually boredness doesn't happen without a fixed location.

I noticed that when my writing stopped, I would look up and see all the creative people around me in Garosugil.

Their creativity would get me thinking a bit (Oh, that's a funny hat), and then I'd get back to what I was doing.

I don't claim to be an extremely creative person. But I think I just learned to be slightly more.

When the Going Gets Tough, the Tough Get Going

GRIT IS A concept made famous by Angela Duckworth in her book *Grit: The Power of Passion and Perseverance*. To be honest, I never read the book because I didn't need justification that grit was important. I was trained that way, and the results have proven its worth firsthand.

Everything in military boot camp is hard. At wake-up, someone is already in your face screaming, close enough to smell your morning breath. As much as you get your uniform on right, drill sergeants will intentionally rip you to shreds to bring you down. Even when you close the toilet stall doors and think you may have some respite to squeeze one out, someone is knocking for you to hurry up so he can go.

Aug 19, 2017

How to Develop Grit

https://thetaklo.medium.com/
how-to-develop-grit-7a748fcfaeac

Grit is the ability to stay confident, cognitively process, and execute actions despite present disadvantages and an unprojectable future. Present disadvantages include pain but also include lacking capital and human resources. All futures are to some degree uncertain, but an unprojectable future is a future that seemingly cannot be projected from the present. Developing grit is a consistent exposure to experiences where the future is unprojectable and present disadvantages are high.

Grit is a learned habit. The more experience one has with present disadvantages and an unprojectable future, the more one can learn to be confident and develop grit. If grit is exercised on a daily basis, grit can be incrementally increased over the long term.

The Army teaches grit at every possible teaching moment. The organization has realized that the faster grit becomes instinctual for an individual, the more likely grit will manifest in the toughest conditions. During basic training, the drill sergeants rarely tell recruits any information, the objective or the mission, to instill the comfort of not knowing an end-goal. Furthermore, drill sergeants deliberately present disadvantages by sleep and food deprivation and pairing weakest soldiers with the best.

I believe the best way to develop grit is to batch the learning process. A short period, say 3 months, of grit-intense experiences develops the habit more effectively than a longer duration of grit-light experiences. The cumulative daily exposure to intense grit is far more effective learning than a period of infrequent grit.

When everything is hard, you develop your grit muscle. Simple as that.

Developing grit is not normal. Unless one is a masochist, most people would not sign up to experience grit and a hard life.

It's just not natural.

So founders have to get out of their way to develop their grit. Because the more grit muscle you have, the more you are willing to take risks. The grittier you are, the more you can handle risk and reap its benefits, and not crumble from its negatives.

Oct 12, 2017

The Importance of Risking Again and Again

*https://thetaklo.medium.com/
the-importance-of-risking-again-and-again-e995852e9ba6*

Risk means different things to different people. For the investor, risk means return. For the older person, risk means unnecessary danger. For the young person, risk means adventure. For me, risk means an opportunity for intense growth.

When you risk something, you abandon the old state for an improved, hopefully better future state. A gambler risks it all to have a much larger payoff than what she is doing now. A non risk-taker is comfortable with the current status quo, not willing to abandon it for the future.

The best case scenario is that the risk pays a huge output. But more importantly, it's important to examine the inputs; risk taking requires a massive amount of effort, taking up enormous energy, intellect, and resources to make sure the risk plays out well. Non risk-taking requires minimum effort; no additional energy or resources is required. That delta equals a dramatic difference in growth because of the effect of gathering and processing all the resources.

Risking again and again allows growth again and again. There is always a finite time when growth is stalled, or the growth cycles have a longer span, but it's important to not abandon risk, because that would mean abandoning growth.

You develop grit by eating more grit. And again and again.

But what you discover is that after a bit of grit, hard things aren't as hard as they once were. Your tolerance for hard work increases. Like alcohol tolerance, your baseline increases slightly.

So you do something harder. And so on and so forth, until you look back at your former self, wondering how you've made such a change, your broad shoulders ready to effortlessly support your problems and those of your loved ones.

∞

In order to develop the grit muscle, I try to classify problems as good or bad. Not all problems are bad, and shouldn't be viewed as such.

If a leader can classify more bad problems as good problems, perhaps working on the grit muscle would be considered more of a joy than a burden.

Aug 9, 2017

Mo' Problems, Mo' Problems

*https://thetaklo.medium.com/
mo-problems-mo-problems-3ba545e8ca98*

*I love problems. My philosophy is that the
sooner I can encounter the problems, the
faster I can go about solving them. There is
nothing worse than encountering a problem
later, the problem debt has stacked up,
and it's even harder to solve the problem.
I genuinely get upset if I don't forecast
a problem I should have seen.*

*There are good and bad problems. Good
problems help further the mission, whereas
bad problems digress or even sink the
mission. Bad problems can be turned around
to be good problems if they serve to further
the mission.*

*Loving problems is a virtuous circle. The
faster you solve those problems, the more
you are able to see other problems and solve
them, and so on and so forth. Over time,
the faster rate of problem solving enables*

any team to be more agile and reactive to change. In a startup, that adaptability and reactiveness is key to survival.

Orienting a culture to solve problems can be achieved in a few ways. One method is to always start and end a discussion with "What are our problems?" and "Did we solve our central problems?" Another is to celebrate individuals that surface problems, rather than the traditional way of hiding problem makers. Third is to get the group to practice and celebrate problem solving, by surfacing group problems and enlisting others' feedback on those problems.

The CEO should be the chief problem maker. If CEOs create lots of problems, that means the CEO is pushing the envelope on the mission, where the startup can go, and the team on solving problems. If not, the CEO is not pushing enough.

A CEO can also help their team develop grit, something I will address later in the blog post "Team + Tension."

∞

Another way to develop the grit muscle is by increasing intensity. It's like a CrossFit workout, where you decrease the time and increase the load to achieve more in a certain amount of time.

And unlike a CrossFit workout, you won't be throwing up.

Aug 7, 2017

The Intensity X-Factor
https://thetaklo.medium.com/
the-intensity-x-factor-cd76840f0181

I learn more when an experience is intense. Intensity entails time shortening, which necessitates faster decision making, which sets a pattern of rapid decisions, feedback, and learning. Furthermore, intensity creates additional stress, which teaches an ability to manage stress and one's reaction to stress.

There are two ways to increase intensity. One is to decrease the amount of time available,

> *while keeping constant the tasks and decisions that need to be made; the other is the opposite and keeping constant time, but increasing tasks and decisions. Of the two, the former is more powerful.*
>
> *Intensity also hedges against procrastination. Human nature is to procrastinate until the last minute, which isn't necessarily a bad thing in that it creates time for brainstorming and examining all options. By being comfortable with intensity, one can allow procrastination until the very last minute, and execute with intensity when needed.*

Intensity is a great thing. It maximizes learning and feeling in the shortest amount of time possible.

Leaders sometimes get addicted to intense situations. But that's not a bad thing either.

Imagine a professional athlete, a Joe Montana or a Kobe Bryant. Because he has been exposed to countless intense situations, he knows precisely what to do at the most critical times. He has trained his ability to focus and execute when the pressure is highest. He has his wits while others are flailing from the pressure.

Imagine a military commander in the fog of war. He waits and waits until he has all the information, gathering data points until the very last moment. That last piece of information may even be the most critical piece of information. And now he has it, a little bit smarter than his enemy.

The Unknown Unknowns

SPEAKING OF THE fog of war, this concept was first mentioned in Carl von Clausewitz's timeless war manual, *On War*. In it, he describes war as "the realm of uncertainty; three quarters of the factors on which action in war is based are wrapped in a fog of greater or lesser uncertainty. A sensitive and discriminating judgment is called for; a skilled intelligence to scent out the truth."

Breaking forth from that uncertainty is the role of a skilled leader.

Jan 25, 2017

Searching for Simplicity

*https://thetaklo.medium.com/searching-for-simplicity
-6cd5580e6d21*

I'm a big fan of finding the simple solution in things. Part of it is searching for elegance. Part is my thesis that most complex things can be distilled to 1 or 2 levers that really impact 80% of the situation. But what happens when there really isn't a perceived simple solution?

That can happen when the situation isn't fully developed. There's simply not enough transparency and information out in the open for there to be a perceived simple solution.

Military strategists call this the fog of war. Information, misinformation, and lack of information accumulates, and complexity increases. The perceived simple solution is hidden by cognitive overload. Decision making is paralyzed.

One solution is to accelerate the situation so that information is apparent. For me the fastest way to do this is to talk to as many people as possible; I did something similar when I first moved back to Asia.

Another way is to establish a time limit on when a decision has to be made. What this essentially does is work backward from the end, and forces an individual to cognitively let go of the fact they don't have enough information, and thus have to come up with the most simple solution they can given constraints.

Sometimes a simple elegant answer isn't the answer. Sometimes the answer is to get your hands dirty and just finish the job.

When in the fog of war, simplicity is best. Simplicity in decision-making, simplicity in getting information, and simplicity in answering. Don't be too clever or elaborate or try to force expectations to conform to the present.

Let the present guide the future.

It's important to note that a leader will never break out of the fog of war completely because the fog is ever-present. The best a skilled leader can do is try to make the best decisions they can and learn from them.

∞

Information gathering is critical in the fog of war. By gathering as much information as possible, you create opportunities for leverage, where you put maximum force on the angle of attack when you act.

That's where you leverage the fog of war to your advantage, because the fog of war doesn't apply only to you; it applies to your competitors too.

It's easy to forget that other people are figuring out the moving landscape as much as you are.

Feb 8, 2017

Isolate and Leverage

Breaking through the next level in life can be difficult. People are slowed down by friction from existing expectations, environment, and externalities. Some of the friction can also be attributed to one's own demons and low expectations. But breaking through is not impossible through a technique called isolate and leverage.

The best way to isolate is to gather as much information as possible. Like water flowing across rocks, the idea is to find and isolate where the water is getting through the rocks. In jiu jitsu, the player takes what the game is giving her, and hones in on the location for maximum leverage.

Then the isolated point is used for maximum leverage. In the water example, it's time to take a jackhammer and push down on the weak spot. In the jiu jitsu example, it's taking the entire body's force and leveraging the weak spot.

This is similar to the tai chi fighting principle "Lead them to emptiness," which I mentioned earlier. But in this case, when you're "leading," you're really listening to them first (a method known as teng jing , 听劲, or listening energy).

You listen to what the external force is saying. You listen so that you don't resist strongly; just enough so the external force encounters a bit of resistance and doesn't sense that you have caved. You have to listen well and constantly be in this Goldilocks state: not too much, not too little.

And when the external force has given you enough and you've listened to your limit, you act.

∞

In the fog of war, decision-making frameworks are critical. They are important so that when the time comes, there are no surprises. It's about eliminating risk and improving mental capacity on difficult decisions. It's about pre-deciding, so that all mental capacity is focused on making the right decision. It's a mental checklist that you can stupidly check off, because your brain won't be able to handle that much more when you're in a high-pressure situation.

In essence, it's like doing all your hard training first so that you can have joy in gametime. So that you can be free in the moment.

Nov 18, 2017

A Framework for Making Difficult Decisions
https://thetaklo.medium.com/a-framework-for-making-difficult-decisions-e996a56aa3f5

Thanks Miles Wen, Keegan Huang, Jia Huang Ho, and Rodolfo Rosini for comments.

I recently had to make a decision that I deemed to be very difficult, at that moment. The ramifications of that decision were too uncertain to forecast, the stakeholders associated with that decision were hard to decipher, and there was no other model that existed, that I know. There was no time urgency, however.

It's important to have such a framework. By having a pre-existing framework in your arsenal, you know you will be able to make a high-quality decision every single time, regardless of time or other pressures. As your experience increases, the framework gets better and the higher quality the decision-making framework is, even with time pressure.

I distilled some principles from that experi-ence, and the other times I've had to address similarly difficult decisions.

Go with the flow, and deal with the situation as it is, as it flows.

Follow your process. The only thing you can control is your process, not the results.

Isolate the key variables in this decision— what are the key drivers to this decision that are more important than the other variables?

Stretch the process out as long as possible, to its maximum limit, in order to gather as much information as possible.

Make the best decision based on two principles: 1) survival and/or 2) what's truly important to you. Having both is the optimal scenario, but if not, 1) is more important than 2).

Deal with the criticism as there will inevitably be many. Incorporate the valid criticism into your mental framework for the next time you make a decision, and disregard the crap.

Move on. Next decision please.

Looking backward, those other difficult decisions deemed to be difficult were indeed difficult and there was no other way I could have made it easier. But each experience was an opportunity to contribute to my mental framework on how to make hard decisions. Furthermore, each experience is evidence that despite a decision being difficult, it never really is life or death; in other words, each opportunity is an opportunity to train resilience.

Having a mental framework is great, but having just one or two things in that framework is even better. Keep it simple when it really matters.

Embrace each decision and each experience as a way to battle-test and upgrade your framework. So that when it really matters, that framework is as perfect as can be.

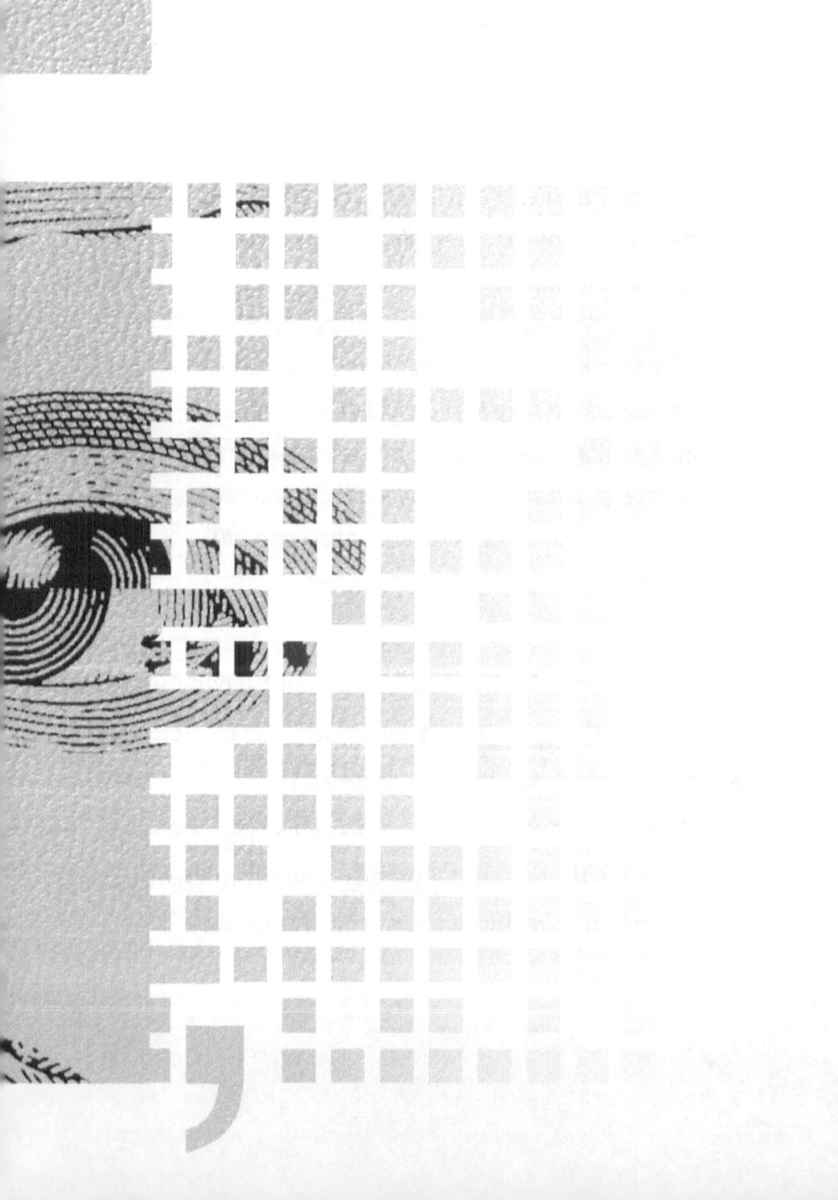

Lead Me, Follow Me, or Get the Hell Out of My Way

I ADMIRE FOUNDERS.

They are, in Theodore Roosevelt's words, the "men in the arena." The ones fighting the war. The ones in the trenches, having to make difficult decisions to kill their baby, the feature they slaved over night and day over a two-week sprint. The ones who might have to fire their best friend to save the company. The ones who are jaded over investors who say they're insanely interested in their round, only to disappear after the third email and fourth iMessage.

I admire their courage the most. Perhaps it's the courage I strive to have myself, causing me to seek others with the same courage muscle.

To seek my own tribe, if you will. I believe that we can all learn from each other and train our courage muscles together.

Because the world needs a bit more courage.

November 22, 2021

Leading

It's a privilege to lead a company, a group,
a mission or just a number of people.
I don't think there's a better vocation
than to lead.

People think it's glamorous to lead. Not
so—leading is oftentimes a lonely vocation.
You have to come in every day and grind
it out, spending time by yourself when the
entire world depends on you. You alone have
to make those decisions that may impact
people's lives.

Leading is believing in the best in people. You have to default to thinking that people are capable of completing a task or accomplishing their responsibility. You have to give faith to people; to believe in the opposite is to set up people for failure.

Leading is thinking long term. Leading in the short term can be painful, with personality conflicts, late deadlines, and missed opportunities. But leading is thinking what the goal is further down the line, and building up tolerance for short-term turbulence.

Leading is welcoming conflict. Leading people will always cause inherent friction, leading missions will always have friction before inertia starts. Leading is welcome that initial conflict as if an old friend. Leading strong personalities is a great thing, for it makes me a stronger leader.

Leading is self discovery. The more you lead, the more you learn about yourself, your weaknesses, your strengths, and your position of impact. Leading forces you to open up yourself to change so that you can make a better impact.

Leading is making mistakes. Fundamentally, you can't learn to be a leader without leading, and that means making mistakes as a leader. Leading is also about trying different things, learning from them, and iterating faster.

Leading is changing the world. There are no innovative efforts without someone leading and changing, despite the status quo. Leading is taking the initiative and wanting to produce some change.

Leading is facing your biggest fears. You don't know half the stuff you should when you lead. You don't know the goal when you do, and half the time the goals keep on changing. And there are still a ton of unknowns left to decipher. But leading is going forward, despite not knowing.

Leading is doing something bigger than yourself. You no longer put yourself and your interests above the group, in fact, you can't. The group, company, and mission has to be

> *bigger. You have to sacrifice and subsume
> your own ego.*
>
> *Leading isn't a natural state to be in. But
> the longer you are in it, the more you
> realize it's not so uncomfortable. Comfort is
> a function of how long you are in that state,
> and the more time you spend being a leader,
> the more you are used to it.*
>
> *Leading is a privilege. Welcome to
> being a leader.*

Leading is loving.

My friend and Techstars LP Doug Scott asked me years ago why I did what I did, what drove me. I didn't quite know what to make of the question, and knowing Doug, who is a bit of a British nutter, I dismissed it.

But after a few months thinking about other things, his comment popped back into my head. *What does drive me? Why do I sacrifice myself, my energy, and my family? What is my why?*

It's because I love founders. I love what they do. And you can't lead without love.

∞

Being a leader can be lonely. There are certain decisions that only you can make—like firing team members—that will be universally derided, no matter how humane the process was or who did the firing. It's very hard for a leader to have people in the organization to speak to.

Equally, there are positives to leadership and managing people. To see their growth as colleagues and as people. To drive forward a vision from nothing and have it impact the world.

Negative and positive are two sides of the same coin. All it takes is a different perspective.

In that vein, it's important to look at things as joys. Because being a CEO often feels joyless.

Feb 16, 2017

The Joy of Being CEO

Being CEO means that you are responsible for the journey and safety of those that entrust you with their passion, focus, and

> *time. This is an awesome responsibility but a joyful one as well.*
>
> *It's a joy to see people achieve things they never thought possible.*
>
> *It's a joy to take people to places they never thought possible.*
>
> *It's a joy to lead the creation of something new and know we willed it into being.*
>
> *It's a joy to think about deep problems and work on them.*
>
> *It's a joy to feel alive with the varying emotions it takes to be CEO.*
>
> *It's a joy to put in a good, honest day's work and say we made an impact.*

Always look for the joy. It's there somewhere, perhaps even a sliver, if you look hard enough.

∞

No leader wants to fail. But at the same time, failure is life. We fail every day: fail to wake up at the right time, to remember something, to not be the standard that we hold ourselves to. Being alive means failing constantly.

We should learn to love our failures. Love them, embrace them, hug them. They are what makes us us.

Because only by owning your failures can you claim them, process them, and clear them away for new growth.

Nov 15, 2017

The Courage in Fixing Failure

https://thetaklo.medium.com/the-courage-in-fixing-failure-7dde7a65d0cf

Thanks Frédérique Mittelstaedt and 张家豪 for comments

Failure should be a part of life, and for founders it is a key part of life. Failure has now been given an over-glamorized reputation; the thinking has shifted over to celebrating failure, as if the courage comes from the willingness to fail. I think this is wrong.

Recently, a third-party person inappropriately discussed certain terms of agreement between founders. These terms were not even accurate, but the perception it created made the relationship tenuous. The agreement became impossible to push through. The third party, rather than exhibiting the courage to try to fix the result, faded into the background.

Failure should be a constant in everyone's lives. It should be as constant as eating in the morning, showering, and going to sleep. As toddlers stumble and fall every so often and say the incorrect words for things they mean, failure should be seen as an opportunity to try something new and find the right solution. The faster you fail, the faster you get to the right thing. Constant failure should be the baseline expectation for someone who wants to optimize learning.

Once failure becomes a constant, then failing as an act itself exhibits no courage. When toddlers stumble and fall and fail at every opportunity, they're seen to exhibit normal, toddler-like behavior of failing, not courage. And as adults, if we shift our thinking that failure is normal, then it no longer becomes courageous to fail.

So in this new state of failure as the norm, courage comes into the picture as the ability to fix failure. It's when something does screw up and the deal goes south, that the party that screwed it up acknowledges his/her role and tries to fix the situation to a place where it wouldn't be considered a failure to all stakeholders. It's the ability to look failure straight in the eye and have the courage to take ownership of the problem. It's the creativity and the courage to apologize to the parties involved and find a solution that appeases some of the desired end-state.

An organization can institute this new set of standards by doing two things. One is to encourage failure, almost to the point of too much; ie. constantly ask the question, how do we push what we're doing to the brink of failure, and then do exactly slightly more than that. This is necessary to make failure the norm, not the exception. Two, it's to detach the process of failing with the result. A good process is pushing to the point where things could fail; the result is an indicator of what should be done to fix the process so that it doesn't fail the next time.

We fail every single day. We should all be more accepting of each other's failures, not to the point of pride, but as acceptance of what it represents as a person's authentic self.

I trust a person who has battle scars. She doesn't need to ram them down my throat, but she shouldn't necessarily hide them either.

Failures exist and form who she is; they allow her to create meaning and narrative. That meaning becomes stories and lessons other people can learn from, enriching their lives too.

Teamwork Wins Championships

EVER SINCE MY military days, it's been important to me to put the team first.

I know how beautiful things can be when people put aside their egos to do one common thing, and everyone gets satisfaction and fulfillment from that one thing. It is only by placating one's ego and serving a higher purpose that we become better humans, whether that purpose is spiritual or mission-oriented.

One of the CEO's jobs is to create great teams, and the most important way to create a great team is to build trust. Not only trust in the leader, but trust as a core cultural characteristic throughout the whole organization.

Jan 7, 2017

Trust

Trust is where one person believes in another person's ability to do the right thing. It can also mean a relationship between one brand or startup to another. It is the one social glue that binds relationships.

Trust is a composition of one's integrity, what one thinks, what one says, and what one does. There is some truth to the saying:

Watch your thoughts, they become words;

watch your words, they become actions;

watch your actions, they become habits;

watch your habits, they become character;

watch your character, for it becomes your destiny

The fundamental principle of this ranking order is integrity. Without integrity as the fundamental Jenga building block, the other actions cannot flow from an integral space. Without that integral space, all the rest is just a facade waiting to come crashing down.

It's hard to align all those above things, but the people that I see do the above well are the ones that keep things simple and transparent. They usually say what they mean. They usually are responsive. They usually don't overthink things. Some people call that authenticity, but I think simplicity is the right word. There is also truth to the lyrics of the folk song "Simple Gifts."

Trust goes both ways in a relationship. You have to give it and have it. I find it easier to give trust first, because that is firmly in my control. Having trust is not within my control, and that takes different amounts of time for different people.

But there are times when you need to prove trust quickly. If there is a sinking ship, a rescuer will demand that a rescuee trust him or her. Of course there is no other option, but that's one way to build trust quickly—by leveraging opportunities that demand trust.

> *Another way to build trust quickly is for others to say you're trustworthy. This only starts a relationship, though, and isn't long-term sustainable; the above alignment of integrity, thoughts, words, and actions needs to be there.*

Trust is the only currency that is constant. Make sure what you say and what you do are exactly aligned.

I know in this day and age it may be hard to do so. But you have to get this right.

∞

Though the mission is important, camaraderie is just as important. Contrary to popular opinion, most soldiers don't actually fight for a cause—they fight for the people to the left and right of them.

So as much as it's important to have great mission and vision statements, it is also important to make sure the bonds between people are healthy and strong. That is what carries a team.

Feb 17, 2017

Camaraderie

Camaraderie is formed when people spend time working together on hard problems or tasks.

If problems were easy, the sense of community wouldn't be as strong because the strength of the task is correlated with its binding power. If the problems are hard, people are forced to rely on each other for help, thus binding them.

If the time spent together were short, likewise the sense of community likely won't be as good if the time spent was longer. But overall between time spent and hard tasks/problems, the stronger weighting has to go to hard tasks/problems.

Camaraderie is a powerful motivator. A mission is likely the best motivator, because it compels an individual personality to align with a goal, but camaraderie is

> *a close second. If you know the other person is working hard, you're likely going to work hard together to pass the time better.*
>
> *Camaraderie can rewire the brain. People are inherently self-interested, but camaraderie can force people to put the group first. This is likely a function of how difficult a task is, rather than time spent together.*

When I look back at my Army times, the people I remember are my squad and my platoon. I am proudest of our times together, when we suffered and when we laughed as a group.

Similarly, your team will only remember who they were with. The company and its values will only be one aspect, and a fading one.

We are only human at the end of the day. And we resonate with fellow humans.

∞

Culture is incredibly important. When you're building a firm or a startup, it's what defines you when nothing else does. It's what keeps people aligned to something. It's what Covid destroyed with remote working, and what everyone is now trying to bring back.

I spend a lot of time thinking about culture because it is so much more important in venture funds and accelerators. It is the integral but non-obvious fascia that binds the portfolio companies and partners together. With culture, a group of individuals are rowing together, working together, winning together.

Jan 6, 2017

Culture
https://thetaklo.medium.com/culture-5899d5b34c05

Culture is defined as the shared experiences, knowledge, norms, and language between a group of people. That group of people can be an organization, a team, a family, or even a society. For today's analysis I'll think of culture from a startup perspective.

There is no inherent right or wrong culture. Every startup has their own unique ways of being, forged through time and practicality. Thus, though there are best practices in building culture, those best practices are at best suggestive, not prescriptive.

Culture morphs through time and mass. As you develop over time or have more people, your culture should change. If it doesn't, something is wrong and you're likely hanging on to something in the past.

Culture is composed of the daily stuff and the big stuff. The daily stuff reinforces certain behaviors and makes culture consistent. The big stuff are the life changing events; things that question one's own existence. The big stuff pulls people together and changes culture in a big way. The key is to turn those things into positive, learning experiences.

I think that's how culture is built—through the big things and reinforcement through the daily things. The big things swing the culture one way or the other way. The small things reinforce those learnings; like someone once said, culture isn't what you say—it's what you tolerate.

> *Culture is helped by a strong founder who has a well defined view on the world. That may be a wrong view and subsequently the wrong culture, but that is exponentially better than having no view or no culture. A strong culture allows momentum and a team to grow, and no culture doesn't allow any of this.*
>
> *A strong culture is hard to define and quantify. Sometimes it's artifacts like a physical office, books, etc. Sometimes it just feels different. I have yet to know how to define it and even value the impact it has.*
>
> *But not knowing how to value it doesn't detract from how important I think it is. Good culture makes people responsive and productive. Good culture scales to different teams and geographies. Good culture can recruit people that you didn't think you could recruit. Good culture is the social glue, the mission we all want in life.*

Culture is easiest to get right in the early days of a startup. When the startup is larger and starting to decentralize, culture can start to fray.

I admire startup cultures with remote teams first. I think they're more effective because they deal with building startup culture on hard mode first. But if they get over the hump, they ultimately scale better.

∞

But how do you get to good culture? Controversially, I think tension is the key.

Tension in a team is important because it keeps everyone on their toes. It surfaces honesty about each team member's intentions, so there is no safe space for ulterior motives. If used correctly, it ensures that the best ideas surface, not just the most popular ones.

And if there is internal tension, and if that tension is properly worked through and massaged out like scar tissue, then the muscle becomes stronger and more prepared to face the harsh outside world.

August 30, 2016

Team + Tension

We had a great team scrum today. It was one of those chats where everyone understood everything, we all knew who was going to do what, and we knew what to really focus on. It was close to a scenario where I felt the team was really in sync and getting each other.

Getting to that team point requires tension. Tension can be manifested early on through debate of ideas, crazy schedules, or any other type of conflict. I feel we had lots of tension early on, which is why we are good now.

Don't fear building tension in the team. Instead, fear not building *enough* tension.

In the Army we used to say, "The more you sweat in training, the less you bleed in battle." This idea holds when it comes to not building enough tension inside the team.

∞

I am drawn to stories of businesses and families that have thrived through not decades, but centuries.

The post below is a reference to a book on the Rothschilds that highlights important characteristics I feel all cultures should have. This family's survival and ability to thrive for so many generations, through wars and economic and political crises, provides some important lessons that are applicable to any startup culture.

Apr 29, 2017

History, Value, and Doing the Right Thing

I'm currently reading The House of Rothschild, Volume I, *about the rise of the world's richest family from the years 1798 to 1848. It's a mighty book—not only because of Niall Ferguson's total command of the facts that surround seminal events in the Rothschilds' history, but his ability to zoom macro and extrapolate trends and themes, and tie them to history. Simply a brilliant piece of work, and a skill I hope to emulate.*

One of themes I've been left to ponder is the importance of being on the right side of history. Those that do end up being identified as part of history's victors; those that don't end up being bit players in somebody else's history.

Another theme is the importance of values. For the Rothschilds, that main value was unbreakable unity, and that value has helped them endure likely more than any other factor, at least in Volume I. What was surprising is that the Rothschilds were never visionary capitalists, but instead opportunistic, from embracing government finance, railway finance, and finally investing in developing countries. That unbreakable unity, however, is what allowed them to ride the revolutionary wave in 1848, survive, and prosper over time.

The third theme is being mission-oriented to do the right thing. The Rothschilds were actually extremely pacifist and concerned for

> *the Jewish cause, and though they weren't as overt as some would like, they did their utmost to preserve their heritage and contribute to its cause. In many respects, I draw the same energy from wanting to advance openness in AI, to bring about material changes in innovation in a field that will dominate our field in the next 50 years.*

The concept of an unbreakable unit speaks to me.

You hear of yet another tech company firing yet another 10 percent of its workforce. You see those "made redundant" videos on Tik Tok. All sides point fingers at each other, but no one quite hits the nail on the head on why this is an issue.

I know why.

When did it all become scaling quickly, and then firing so fast? When was firing over email or Slack okay? What happened to morale, culture, and team? What happened to humanity?

It's not surprising that we in the tech world fear AI. It's because we've lost our own humanity.

We lost it in the pursuit of perfection. In the pursuit of optimization. In the pursuit of technocratization.

Artificial intelligence, like any technology before us, only amplifies and reveals more of what we truly are. Only this time, AI has truly looked into our soul and questioned our own humanity, or lack thereof.

AI can help us look into our own souls and reveal a brighter boulevard, or a dark descent. The choice is ours to make. The orientation is ours to face.

So in this age of AI, humans still matter. Human leadership matters. Humans lead.

That mission is still alive and well, and I hope to continue leading the way for the next 50.

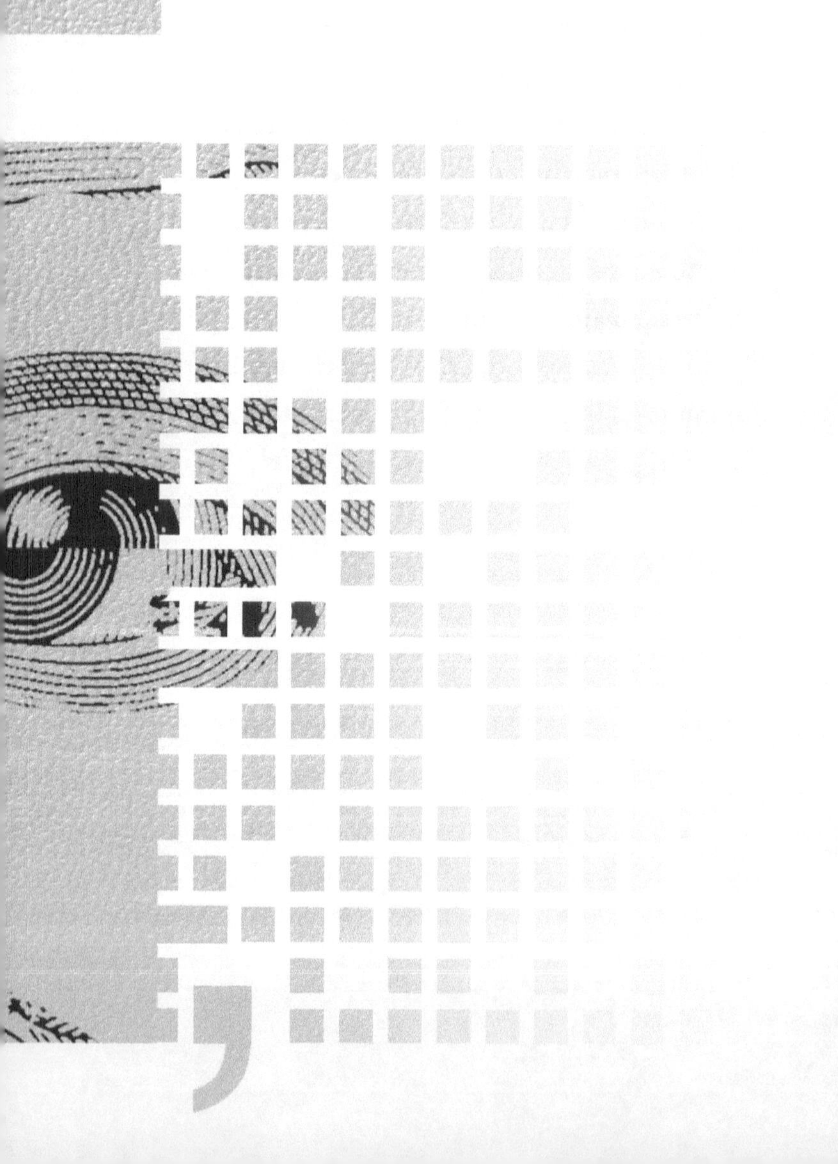

Postscript

THESE LAST SECTIONS are much more tactical in nature. They describe the two things I was doing at the time of formulating the above leadership lessons: building the AI accelerator and evaluating the Chinese tech ecosystem.

In "How to Build an Accelerator," I discuss my thoughts on building the program, from deal flow to decision-making to mentoring. For those looking to build an accelerator program from scratch, this is an intimate, firsthand monologue on building one. It's the essence of my experience building a program after learning from the best.

In "China AI Ecosystem," I discuss what I learned about the Chinese ecosystem and AI, and where it might go. I remain interested in China and its standing in the world, and think this section will interest those who think similarly.

How to Build an Accelerator

AN ACCELERATOR IS just another name for an early-stage venture capital fund, one with a structured program that allows a firm to deploy and work with startups at scale. As of the writing of this book, there are over 2,000 accelerators in the United States alone.

Paul Graham launched the first accelerator, Y Combinator, in 2005, with Sam Altman from now OpenAI famously being part of his first cohort, as well as Reddit's Alexis Ohanion. In 2006, seeking to replicate the magic that is Silicon Valley, David Cohen approached Brad Feld to create a mentor-based accelerator model in Boulder, which effectively builds startup ecosystems in places that do not have any. And in 2010, Dave McClure and Christine Tsai took yet another approach to the accelerator model with 500 Startups, scaling the program internationally, establishing accelerators firmly as a global phenomena.

I have honed my craft with the best. I joined one of the largest accelerator programs in the world with Techstars at the tail end of 2012, first in New York with Nicole Glaros, who was with Techstars right from the beginning in Boulder with David Cohen and Brad Feld. Then I helped Jon Bradford and Jess Williamson build Techstars London, the first international program and the first in Europe.

My accelerator education didn't stop there. I got to see how our program compared to others in the European scene, like Seedcamp, Entrepreneur First, the Family, and direct competitor YC in the Valley.

When I moved to Asia, other programs wanted to recruit me, but I didn't see how my career would progress as I wouldn't be running the program directly and only working in the background.

So I decided to start my own. I raised funding from Dave McClure at 500 Startups, so I could closely follow what they did and their learnings.

I wrote the following post to recap some of the lessons I had learned working with and observing some of the top accelerators in the world. It was a time of reflection right before we started, and I wanted to make sure I understood all the elements of what makes a world-class accelerator, at least conceptually.

Sept 19, 2016

What I've Learned from Building an AI/ML Accelerator from the Ground-Up

https://thetaklo.medium.com/what-ive-learned-from-building-an-ai-ml-accelerator-from-the-ground-up-5d7882090bca

Just 5 months ago we started Zeroth. And this Sunday, September 25 will be the application deadline for my first cohort.

I'm experienced with accelerator programs. Before Zeroth, I was at Techstars, first in New York and then starting the first international Techstars program in London alongside Jon Bradford and Jess Williamson. Through that experience, I worked with over 50 startups, managed over 120 mentors, and hired over 40 Associates and Hackstars. I also helped out and knew other accelerators well, including Spark Labs, Startup Wise Guys, 500, Seedcamp, Eleven, ERA, How to Web, ChinaAccelerator, Oxygen and others.

I went through an accelerator withdrawal phase. After Techstars I was a venture partner at Mind Fund, where I focused on working with later stage companies. I increasingly became interested in artificial intelligence and machine learning through my companies Aire, Lingvist, and Weave. But I couldn't shake off my interest in working with early stage companies, especially those at the very infancy. And that's when I married those two interests to form a new vision: to deconstruct, fund, and hyper-accelerate the building of AI/ML startups.

Every accelerator has to solve for the following areas. These areas are pertinent to any investment firm, whether it be tech or not, but for simplicity I'll only address accelerators:

Brand: *Brand is the precursor to deal flow; if you have a great brand, there are a few areas where deal sourcing is improved: more inbound deals come your way and a higher conversion of those inbounds to completed deals.*

Coming from Techstars, the brand issue was very much solved. When you're building an accelerator from scratch, a brand has to be formed.

Deal Flow Process: *The process to actually find companies*

Operations Process: *The team also had to run operations optimally.*

Due Diligence Process: *How to perform due diligence on startups.*

Brand

An accelerator brand comprises its community of portfolio companies. But without a portfolio to start from, an accelerator has to build its brand on the strength of its team and the companies that the team has been involved with.

That's why we assembled one of the best lineups of AI/ML entrepreneurs and venture capitalists, including Jaan Tallinn, cofounder of Skype, Nathan Benaich from Playfair Capital, Frank Meehan from Spark Labs, Jung Hee Ryu of FuturePlay, Daniel Chu from Microsoft Cortana, Thomas Stone from Prediction.io, Azeem Azhar from Exponential View, and others. In aggregate, this team has worked with companies like Google DeepMind, Siri, Mapillary, Vicarious, Seldon, Weave, and other important AI companies.

Deal Sourcing Operations

The success of an accelerator relies on its ability to attract companies, or its deal sourcing. Every accelerator has its own sourcing tactics depending on the team's value proposition, personalities, geographic focus, market, thesis, and/or stage. As time passes, an accelerator's sourcing

*tactics may change as well to adjust
to the market.*

*The framework that's worked so far is
a two-pronged approach:*

Scaled Sourcing: *Sourcing through actions
or events that influence a large number of
startups at a single point in time*

Referral Sourcing: *Sourcing through
direct referrals from other investors or
community leaders*

Internal Operations

*The accelerator operations have to run
efficiently to optimize for the greatest amount
of value creation with every unit of effort.
Over time, this ratio should increase with
tweaks to the model, but some accelerators also increase value creation via adding
more programs.*

Some of the things we do:

Rely on the aptitude of 1: *In the beginning,
we double-teamed trips and interviews as*

a process of getting to know each other. Now that everyone is competent, we rely on the power of each individual person to make an impact. Emphasizing individual impact forces responsibility, decision-making, and action.

Batching: *We batch process almost everything we do, from recruitment, interviews, value-creation, and fundraising. We offer a fair investment deal and state our terms up front so that we waste no time negotiating terms, and spend more time on value-creating actions.*

Layering: *We layer on top of existing investment, social, physical, or other networks. No need to waste time recreating networks if they are already there.*

Due Diligence Process

How an accelerator selects the best startups for its cohort is a combination of rationality and gut-feel. The rational part is gathering and processing the numerous data points and feedback associated with a startup. The gut-feel is that decision-making point, after

*processing all the data points, on which
startup to pick.*

For us, the rational part is:

Documenting the candidate startups: *We
use Streak to annotate startups that we talk
to, but we've heard good feedback about
ProsperWorks and Hubspot.*

**Sustaining the conversation with candidate
startups over a period of time:** *We constantly
ask for micro-updates, whether it's through
email, WhatsApp, Messenger, or any other
mediums. It gives us a picture of progression
over time, not just at one single point in time.*

**Tapping the collective due diligence intel-
ligence:** *We ask the extended Zeroth team to
interview and give feedback on candidates.*

*The gut feel decision-making part we
have yet to do, but some of the things
I've learned is:*

➡️ *Decide based on being able to make an
   impact and add value*

> → *Decide based on non-obvious competitive advantages*
>
> → *Decide based on good teams*
>
> *Jon Bradford—maybe you actually did know what you were doing after all.*
>
> *Thanks to Jon Bradford, Paul Smith, Mike Reiner, Vincent Jacobs, Hussein Kanji, Nathan Benaich, Bill Earner, Rui Ma, and Tytus Michalski for ideas and thoughts.*

When I look back at this post, I realize I had gotten most of these elements and processes correct, and they're applicable to anyone building an accelerator.

The due diligence process was something we did differently at Zeroth than Techstars, where we had conversations earlier with the startups and documented the progress more. This informs our decision-making later, to a much richer degree than just an application form would.

One thing to note that I didn't mention in my blog post was that we wanted to build an accelerator that was focused on decentralization, since it didn't make sense to us why startups would come to Hong Kong to live or stay. As a consequence, we probably created the world's first decentralized remote accelerator program, even before crypto.

∞

For the second cohort, I wanted to pursue a few more accelerator elements that I thought were similar to Y Combinator, including delaying the pitching until the last two weeks, reducing the number of venture partners, and hosting weekly dinners.

Eliminating some of the venture partners was key—it's just incredibly hard to have world-class partners in Hong Kong, and I didn't really want to start using Zoom as I believe mentoring should be a face-to-face experience.

Oct 27, 2017

Learnings from Z02 and Going Forward to Z03

https://medium.com/techburst/learnings-from-z02-and-going-forward-to-z03-8df3d9267d38

Going into Z02, we wanted to try the following things:

→ *Partner with organizations like AWS, Cooley, and SendGrid to provide resources to founders, and MTR who provided video data so that companies could train their algorithms*

→ *Focusing on pitch and strategy in the first two weeks, to align teams to a hypothesis trajectory*

→ *Invite Venture Partners to travel to see the teams in the first two weeks to actively help and probe pitch and strategy*

→ *Migrate team management to Slack and invite all Z02 participants, including venture partners to better facilitate conversations*

→ *Focusing on the quality of venture partners rather than quantity and allowing them to develop deeper connections with teams by facilitating weekly calls*

→ *Host weekly Master Dinners, where the world's best minds contribute and share their knowledge with the founders, so we learn different mental frameworks. Guests include experts in blockchain like Trent McConaghy; Shai Oster, Pulitzer Prize winning journalist at the Information; founder of Araya, a human conscious AI startup, Ryota Kanai; Ben Goertzel, founder of Singularity Net; founder of Sensay, Ariel Jalali; and community development leader Tim Falls.*

→ *Support fundraising by devoting the last two weeks exclusively to pitch preparation, fundraising tactics, and knowledge development*

For the second cohort Z02, we had 12 companies representing 8 countries and 11 industries. They represent the best companies we've had and are tackling important issues. We're super proud of Z02, the bonds they created, and the impact they will create.

Also a big salute to Partners who contributed over 800 hours of mentoring to the founders, and we salute Sachin Unni, Hajime Hotta, Rodolfo Rosini, Alexandre Winter, Eamonn Carey, Takahiro Shoji, Antoine Blondeau, Katherina Lacey, and Phil Chen, Jaan Tallinn, and Chih-Han Yu.

So looking forward to our next cohort Z03, we made some changes to the way we operate.

We will utilize our own algorithm to decide which startups to invest in. We have increased our algorithm to gather 3x more data points to more accurately assess companies. We're excited to be the first AI accelerator program to utilize machine learning in this way. We believe in the power of algorithms, and that all human decision-making can be automated and engineered in an algorithm.

We are actively targeting Areas of Interests (AoI's) in Logistics, Cybersecurity Voice and

Speech/NLP, Agtech, Medtech, Robotics for our application

To support these AoI's, we have increased our partners including: Jung Hee Ryu, partner at Future Play, a leading AI and deep tech VC based in Korea, and successfully exited his computer vision startup to Intel. He will help founders think about the Korean market; Spencer the Steady, cofounded KeyReply, a leading chatbot platform that works with customers like the Government of Singapore, MSIG, Zalora and other enterprises. He was at Twitter and leads AsiaPac for a esports cryptocurrency company—Unikrn; Rui Ma, previously was the China Partner at 500 and helping founders think about the China market and fundraising; Daniel Saito, early investor in Facebook, Asia Pac lead for MySQL, and crypto investor. He will help founders think about ICOs; Jude O'Kelly, partner at Mount Parker Ventures, an early stage HK based fund. He will lead the logistics stream.

We are hosting the first Beijing AI summit on Dec. 7th, where we will showcase the best AI

> *startups both inside and outside China. We*
> *believe that China will be a force and lead*
> *the new AI era.*

We were clever in trying to use machine learning to combine the data that we had on the startup's progress during the due diligence process with the application data.

We were still in the early days, however. I have since heard other startups focus on this machine learning component exclusively.

This was also our first foray into China—and a harbinger of things to come. I certainly recognized in China the immense size of the market and the importance of its ecosystem on a global stage, and that the nature of AI startups to come from there would be different. We ended up investing in just a few Mainland startups.

I hope to change that in the near future.

∞

In 2017, some macro events like ICOs and the Softbank Vision Fund suddenly put a lot of liquidity in the global startup scene.

Looking back, what a wild time that was.

Jan 1, 2018

Annual Report 2017: Eleven Principles for 2018

https://thetaklo.medium.com/ annual-report-2017-eleven-principles-for- 2018-9a86a63f467

If I have a superpower, it is an ability to let go of the past. That ability has allowed me to power through bad experiences, to grow, and to project in the future.

But I have learned to look backward. The holiday season is such a perfect time to embrace the slowness of the seasons, and to chalk the time as a period for self-reflection. And as Winston Churchill puts it—"the farther back you can look, the farther forward you are likely to see."

So looking back on 2017 and the first day for 2018, here are principles from the past and for the future, in the spirit of Ray Dalio's book of the same name.

Thanks to Zeroth founders

Zeroth founders are the lifeblood of what Zeroth is; their success is Zeroth's success, but more importantly, their learnings are Zeroth's learnings. There is no other rule as important.

Eleven principles I've distilled through the course of working with the founders and their companies.

→ **More capital sources, more complexity:** *ICOs as a capital source is here to stay (not the $100m raises, but smaller $5 to $10m), along with larger funds like Softbank and the rumored Sequoia, and corporates getting into the investment game like Japan's banks. There are more capital options available, but more complexity due to new regulations. In other words, mo' money, mo' problems.*

- **Asia rising:** *And not just talking about China. Japan wants to keep competitive, and Korea and Singapore want to stay in the race. Where there's competition, there is energy; and where there is energy, there is opportunity.*

- **Corporates want to play:** *2018 is when AI becomes mainstream in the form of increased corporate activity, in the form of investment and acquisitions. No one wants to miss the opportunity to build AI capabilities into an existing team.*

- **Policy coordination:** *AI mainstream implementation and mistakes of tech companies the skirted regulations will force more high level governmental inter and intra policy coordination. This will require the support of private players with some public policy experience, not the other way around.*

- **Serve customers first, ask later:** *Customers are the lifeblood of any business relationship, and if their interests are served, all else falls in place.*

Once their interests are not served, the fundamentals of business crumble.

➜ **Find patterns, establish them, and test:** *The best innovators are the ones that discover patterns before anyone else makes them a norm. They quickly draw conclusions between different ideas and test them in the market. This could even be drawn into the OODA loop framework, perhaps as an additional step after deciding.*

➜ **In the age of superficial, invest in deep:** *We live in a world where micro-interactions, clicks & tweets, and one-minute attention spans rule; instead, we should turn the cheek and invest our attention in deep interaction, deep work, and deep tech. We're starting to realize the limit of short-term gains, and the pendulum is swinging over.*

➜ **The best relationships are forged from both parties' willingness to learn:** *This goes for every human relationship, whether it be employee, investor, or* *customers. Invest in relationships where both parties want to learn, and end relationships when they don't.*

➔ **Gather the people that believe in you:** *The more successful companies had employees, founders, and investors that really believed in the mission and the founder, despite financial, business, and other risks. If there is belief, enlist; if there is no belief, get rid.*

➔ **At every juncture, find the lesson:** *Some would call this an attitude of optimism, but I feel this is distinct; founders who are able to process any and every event and to learn from it are not merely optimistic, they're learning machines. They are able to add to their repertoire lessons from their past, and in doing so ensure that there is a lower probability that they will make the same mistake again.*

➔ **Follow instincts and project into the future, then back up with action:** *The best founders work on instinct that*

> *a certain move or decision is best, and find a way to make things happen to fulfill the promise of that move or decision. Sometimes they can't verbally explain why a decision is made, other than the intuition that it is correct. The more important lesson is that even if it is the wrong decision, the founder works to make sure the decision ends up well.*
>
> *Lastly, thank you to all our investors, partners, and co-investors. Let's make 2018 a year we create the future we all want to see.*

Unfortunately this is no longer the case—both ICOs and Softbank (later-stage capital) dried up. In fact, the opposite has happened: with interest-rate hikes, the venture capital scene itself dried up. According to one study, venture funding in 2023 was less than half of 2022 levels.

Despite this, I still believe Asia is rising. If you take a look at many GDP projections, by 2050, China,

India, and the US will command between 12 and 15 percent of the world's GDP.

The following blog post was a way to process how different our decision making was in the new Z03 Zeroth cycle. The quality was getting higher, and we were being forced to make harder decisions on which startups to select and which to deny.

I remember sharing this framework with the team so that we could quickly decide which startups to invest in; at the end of the day, making a decision is as much a gut feel as having all the data in front of you.

Mar 5, 2018

Z03 and High Conviction Decision-Making
https://thetaklo.medium.com/
z03-and-high-conviction-decision-making-5ad63496aecd

We start Z03 today. Amongst the feelings of nerves one gets before meeting any new founders, there is a calm in the understanding that this is and will be a unique journey. All cohorts are different in personalities and the differences are what makes the personal growth process fun.

Looking back at the formation of Z03, the one lesson I can isolate is our improved decision making. We realized that conviction is likely the best filter for great founders, and to attract great founders we equally have to display conviction. And in our processes, conviction is the velocity of decision-making, by reducing both the number of steps and time per step to make a decision.

High-conviction decision-making is more effective not only because it attracts the best founders, but also because it forces us to be clearer about our criteria. It forces us to put in work to figure out what we really are looking for, even before we make the actual decision. It forces better cohesion and coordination between all the decision makers, and a tighter feedback loop into what is good and what is bad.

I believe that high-conviction decision-making will be the key differentiator for Z03. Every cohort decision-making process going forward should demonstrate and improve that conviction velocity.

High-conviction decision-making can be a real differentiator in the eyes of a startup founder. It's like the difference between a person you fancy who says "I like you back" right after you text, and someone who gives you an answer that doesn't quite give you the same confidence.

What you want to aspire to is to say "yes" or "no" in the shortest time possible, ideally right after a meeting has ended.

You want to have the confidence that every decision that you make is the true reflection of how you truly feel, without bias or second guessing in the way.

You want purity in thought, and purity in action.

∞

The following blog post was my way to process the proper way to build a firm. The basis of building an accelerator and venture firm is spending a lot of time thinking and gathering expertise in a particular area.

This can often be years or even decades. After all, a firm is in the intellectual capital space, and the practice of knowledge management is the only thing that keeps a firm a firm.

Over the years, I have come to realize that this is the most underrated and hardest part of building a venture firm. It is hard because there really is no deliverable associated with it—unless you count modern venture capital firms where content is now the deliverable. But content for content's sake is not the way to build intellectual capital—content for the firm's sake is the proper way to do so.

It is underrated because everything else in a firm is a derivative of the firm's intellectual capital. How a firm invests, how a firm conducts its operations, and how a firm communicates all stem from how a firm views itself.

September 23, 2016

Building Excellence

I see four ways to build excellence in an investment organization, which is to build aggregate intelligence and experience:

> *A. within one sector or vertical, keeping stage flexible*

> *B. within one sector or vertical, keeping stage fixed*

> *C. across multiple sectors or verticals, keeping stage fixed*

> *D. across multiple sectors or verticals, keeping stage flexible*

Of the four, I see it much more effective to optimize on fixed sector or vertical AND stage (option B). The challenges of the others are:

> *A. This requires networks in upstream and downstream investors and the legal*

> *and operational expertise to add value given any stage.*
>
> *C. This requires operational expertise across sectors, which gets easier as you get later-stage (the value-add is operational efficiency), harder for early stage (value-add is a bigger universe of issues).*
>
> *D. This has the combined difficulty of A and C.*

My opinion of the above has not changed in how to build excellent venture organizations, though I think sector can mean geography as well.

∞

Deal flow is the lifeblood of any accelerator or venture capital firm. From a macro level, deal flow is the supply of companies a VC fund has access to and can therefore invest in. If a VC has great deal flow, then it has the opportunity to invest in great companies that can generate a return. If a VC has terrible deal flow, then the companies are terrible and the returns will likely be so as well.

But if you break down what deal flow really is, at least for an early stage investor, it's the people who you want to be with for the next ten years, at a minimum. These founders are the ones who will be driving the company, their teams, their strategy, and ultimately, your fund's returns.

So it is crucial to figure out the profile of exactly who you want to be with, as early as possible. Thus, as you start scaling and gaining a critical mass of these profiles, the community gets stronger and more clearly defined.

∞

Another thing that we did differently was to appeal to founders who wanted to create a startup but had not thought about AI before.

In essence, I was trying the concept of forcing startups to build from AI first, rather than investing in startups that were already AI. I was trying to have a conversation *earlier* so that I could help *create* AI startups.

There were two reasons why I had to go down this route: one, the deal terms I offered at that time included only $20K per startup, so I was competing with Y Combinator and Techstars, despite my intense focus on AI. In essence, I had to go even earlier and riskier on founders.

Second, this was the place I could create more impact. Investing in early-stage founders allows me and the program to create marginally more impact, as there are fewer stakeholders involved and the product is a lot less mature. In essence, my program's value proposition increases the earlier I focus in the company formation cycle.

July 17, 2016

The Rational Case for Ambition

https://thetaklo.medium.com/
the-rational-case-for-ambition-36f7bbf50fed

I believe in ambition. I like working with ambitious founders because they stretch my imagination and force me to work to be a better version of myself. Founders like Mait from Lingvist and Rodolfo from Weave are prime examples of people who push their visions of the future.

There are practical reasons why founders should be ambitious. Ambitious founders achieve extraordinary outcomes, both economically and socially, compared to un-ambitious founders. Ambitious founders scale faster, saving opportunity cost for themselves, their team, and their investors.

One reason why ambitious founders can do the above is what I call the resource amplification effect. Given two startups with similar start points, for every unit of time, ambitious startups achieve more output because of their ability to command superior resources. In effect, ambitious startups are able to achieve outcomes in a shorter amount of time.

Ambitious founders are able to marshal resources because ambitious employees (human capital) and investors (financial capital) want to work with them. Better employees, due to 10x capabilities, can help a startup build faster with each unit of time. Better investors, due to their experience and networks, can help a startup scale with each unit of time and money.

(Caption: The Resource Amplification Effect of Ambition)

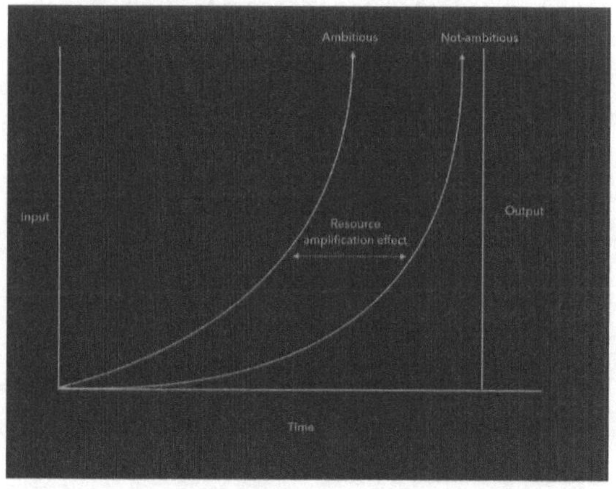

The Chinese AI Ecosystem

I HAD ALWAYS wanted to break into the Chinese market. Hussein Kanji from Hoxton Ventures once told me that there are only two big markets in the world, the US and China, and thus only startups tapping those two markets would be able to provide exceptional returns to a fund. Theoretically and mathematically, I still believe that is true.

Chinese founders have to contend with certain conditions that I find extremely different from anywhere else in the world. For example, there are a lot of tools that are not available in China, and in many ways Chinese founders are handicapped against what they want to accomplish. As a recent example, many

Chinese founders do not have access to ChatGPT, and thus have to use a VPN to access it and other tools such as Google Docs.

There are recent restrictions like the Committee on Foreign Investment in the United States (CFIUS), where Chinese investment in US technology companies is restricted in certain national security use cases, and the reverse for President Biden's 2023 Executive Order, dubbed "reverse CFIUS."

Chinese founders also have to deal with differences in their term sheets compared to their Western counterparts. One is the issue of veto rights, where the current round investor has the ability to veto any new investor coming in. So if a current investor doesn't like the next round investor, she can block that investor's participation.

The second term is the company or the founder having to buy back shares of the investor, within a certain time frame. This allows the investor to make a return, and ostensibly, to be able to make returns for its fund.

A professor I interviewed who has experience both in Beijing and Silicon Valley says that there are fewer entrepreneurs than in the Valley. Or at least they don't share the same ethos where many young people want to be entrepreneurs. I haven't seen enough to verify whether that is true, but in my travels I concluded that the Chinese ecosystem is just as vibrant.

Chinese founders naturally think about scale. The Chinese market is 1 billion people, and as one investor says, it's really thinking about how to scale rather than the market itself. Because trust me, he says, the market is there.

The feedback loop between a startup and consumers is also faster and more direct. Because of social media and a much wider sample size when marketing to a general population of 1 billion, startups can get more direct consumer feedback, allowing them to quickly tweak their product offering and price to better satisfy their customers.

Quick China Thoughts

Currently riding an Uber to dinner. Listening to Jamie Lawson on my desktop Spotify. Operating on SmarTone 3G roaming access with HK servers, so Facebook and Twitter working 100%. I.e., operating with almost 100% efficiency, or even more because I've outsourced my transportation.

I'm much more prepared this trip. I have ExpressVPN so even if I use local wifi I'm connected. I've got SmarTone roaming so my phone has access. 3G and 4G connectivity is great.

There are a lot of reasons why China is scary. It's a totally different startup culture and market than what I'm used to. Out of all the Asian ecosystems I know, I profess to know the least about China. The market is huge and I don't even know where to start.

But in terms of value—there's a ton here. Most founders are first generation, there is tons of capital available, and there is a real hunger to be an entrepreneur. People are open to new ideas and quick to adopt new technologies.

I wasn't expecting that.

September 8, 2016

Beijing Goodness

Currently in Beijing attending the AWS summit. Super interesting to get more plugged into the scene this time around, meet investors from GSR, CGC, and Sequoia, and AI startups large and small, including Cortana's team.

What have I learned about the scene:

- ***There's a shit ton of AI happening here:*** *Most activity is currently on the corporate level (Baidu, Microsoft, etc.) but there are also a ton of startups in the AI space.*

- ***There's a shit ton of capital here:*** *Maybe this isn't a big surprise for most people, but the fact really didn't hit me until I was here*

- ***There's a shit ton of sophistication here:*** *the best investors know a ton about the world. Whether about Pokemon Go (which is banned) or SV investments, the investors and the entrepreneurs know what's going on in the world. Even behind the Great Firewall, the best know what's going on in the world.*

- ***There's a shit ton of data here:*** *This was a point highlighted by Ben, CEO from Liulishuo; that China has a huge concentration of data that only makes AI more interesting*

This won't be the last time we're here. There's too much goodness going on.

This was my first interaction with China as a businessman, so the interface challenge was much more acute. It's hard to describe—you have to be there to see it.

Which points to my own personal journey. Now that I'm going into China, I realize that for a long time I was avoiding doing so because I was scared of the prospect. Which is funny if you think about it—I'm Chinese and I'm scared of going into my own country.

I find going into Beijing or Shanghai extremely intimidating. It's like a totally different culture, with Beijing's power dynamics and Shanghai's old school capitalism. It's not just the language part, which I'm generally okay with, but the whole cultural difference; one way to think about it is that in Beijing or Shanghai, my contributions have very limited value-add to the tech community.

But in the GBA (the Greater Bay Area, not to be confused with the SF Bay Area), I have that value-add. I generally feel more at home, since it's the Southern area of China where Cantonese is spoken, which I speak natively. Secondly, the Southern region has always been more open to the outside, starting with Guangzhou as a foreign trading port in the 17th century. In fact, the word "Canton system" that describes the trading pattern between Chinese and foreign merchants, is aptly named because of the city.

∞

During my time building Zeroth, I wanted to do something in China as a way to learn. So here I have to thank Selina Liu for convincing us to do an event, my first attempt in China. At first I wasn't quite sure what we could do and how it would work, and if we'd be taken to the cleaners if it failed.

But I really liked her idea to host something in China and in particular in Beijing, the seat of power.

Nov 21, 2017

Why We're Doing our Beijing AI Summit
https://thetaklo.medium.com/
why-were-doing-our-beijing-ai-summit-48a7cf9b264

On December 7th, we're hosting the first ever Zeroth AI Beijing summit. We're incredibly excited to host a conversation with AI leaders inside and outside China, and explore the activity there.

We have a deep conviction that China will lead the world in AI in the near future. There are a few arguments for this:

+ ***Human labor is hard to upgrade:*** *to sustain 7% to 8% per annum GDP growth, China needs to improve its labor force and service economy. However, humans and human labor is hard to upgrade, and especially at the pace that China needs. The central government feels that upgrading technology to address some of the increasingly sophisticated service demands is key.*

+ ***Huge data pipeline:*** *With a 1.4 billion population growing at 0.59% per annum, the volume of data generated from a technologically advancing populace is a treasure trove for finding patterns. The Chinese consumer orientation toward data privacy also increases the volume of data available.*

> → **Opportunity to leapfrog:** *China knows that the last three industrial revolutions were a missed opportunity to lead, and China won't let that happen once more. Leading the next generation of technology is a key strategic necessity.*

> *We couldn't be more excited to be a part of the conversation. If you're interested in attending—book here.*

> *I also have to thank Warren Li for doing this. Without him helping out and contributing monetary help we wouldn't have been able to execute.*

And the follow-up post on what we learned.

Dec 11, 2017

What we learned at the Zeroth Beijing Summit

https://thetaklo.medium.com/what-we-learned-at-the-zeroth-beijing-summit-85ee09acdc1a

Biggest thanks goes to the SaasPad team and the leadership of Selina Liu and 小花, who helped us pull off the impossible. The volunteers who did their duty with humor and good fun. Ms Nielixi and the team from Innoway, for their government support and Warren Li, from title sponsor Amazon Web Services. Jonathan Rechtman and the trans-

lation team from Cadence for their profes-sionalism and fun.

The Zeroth Beijing AI Summit was an unequivocal success. The first reason is that we ruthlessly executed to establish a different conversation in China about AI. The second reason is that we showcased some of the best AI companies in the world. The third reason is that we learned about the Beijing and Chinese AI scene in a much deeper and efficient way.

Ruthless Execution

The top-line outcome was the following:

We hosted around 600 people, with over 900 registered attendees.

This is a 66% conversion rate, which is amazing for a mostly free event. This is even more amazing because in the month of December, the event calendar is quite full , and we still managed to attract the audience volume, with marketing of only 2 weeks

Most importantly, we proved that we are serious about our efforts in China. One of our fundamental beliefs is that China will lead AI, and we believed that we had to participate in the conversation about AI. For us, the only right place to do it was in Beijing, the heart of China. And we ruthlessly executed in a country where others fear to tread.

The production quality of the summit was superb. The Chinese/English blend was great, the moderator Jonathan was awesome, we asked insightful questions to our panelists, and we had an incredible format of keynotes, panels, and videos.

Forwarding the conversation

One of our key goals was to push the level of conversation in AI, to bring the best of AI thought leadership to the audience. I think we succeeded.

We hosted over 15 speakers, with topics like:

→ *Investing in AI with top Chinese investors including China Growth Capital's Wayne Shiong, Matrix Partners' Harry Man, and Pre Angel Lizhuohuan*

→ *Rui Ma, Frédérique Mittelstaedt, from Automorph, and Miles H. F. Wen from Fano Labs, where they explored what is different about building and investing in an AI startup.*

→ *AI ethics with Danit Gal, Alex Lin from 价值中国网, and Tencent's Zhoujiecheng on the ethical conversation within China, and how there is an opportunity to shape the conversation via a Chinese or Asian way.*

→ *Future of health with Anne Ma from Shukun and Jiangxun from Yiyun Health, who defined how health is even more specific to different cultures and how health may bring about a much bigger impact in China.*

→ *Brian Chien from IDEO explaining human centric design in an age of more data and automation.*

➤ *Spencer Yang and Jenny Gu talking about defining corporate relationships with startups, how both sides are working more closely together, and will continue to do so.*

➤ *Ryota Kanai about programming human consciousness at Araya, and the complexity of the task.*

➤ *Fred Almeida from Ascent and Pedro Cortez from NavInfo talking about autonomous driving in China and Japan, with a view that China will lead Level 5, and that autonomous cars will increase vehicles on the road, not decrease.*

➤ *Keegan Huang about personified AI and Tammy Yang about AI at the edge.*

➤ *AI trends with Jaan Tallinn and Azeem Azhar, with Jaan sharing a positive opportunity to shape our future and Azeem aggregating macro views to explain the AI explosion.*

China Learnings

We also learned a lot about the developing Chinese ecosystem.

> *Beijing will be the political capital, and the Greater Bay Area will lead innovation.*

> *Already Beijing is making moves to become only the political and cultural capital, with cleaning up the city and moving people away from the center, establishing everything around the 2nd ring as the Central Government seat of power, and cleaning up the air quality by forcing factories to shut down and removing building signs to clear the skyline.*

> *State owned enterprises will be forced to privatize to be more competitive, thus creating an opportunity for startups to work with established players with local resources.*

The AI ethics conversation is only just starting, but inevitably it will be different from the Western AI conversation.

Conclusions

We will continue this conference annually. It is clear that the conversation served a need in this region, and we want to lead that conversation.

China will be a significant player in the AI space. The number of attendees and the sophistication of the current AI players already merit significant attention; with the desire of the central government to transform AI into a $150 billion industry, there will be even more sophisticated AI companies.

Looking back, I'm super impressed by both the lineup of the speakers and the attendance. We filled a massive exhibition center room, with an all English speaker lineup in China!

My learnings and conclusions on AI and its relevance to China have not changed. China wants AI to be a backbone of its technology relevancy, and is currently taking a laissez faire approach to its proliferation. This is akin to the "Let a hundred flowers blossom" strategy.

Because of this approach, I forecast China to be a major player in the AI space. Of course, China will have its own versions of technologies, to onshore this potential and protect it from competitors. And of course, those versions will follow their own development path, though they will also mirror the development of the technology outside of China.

That growth is exciting.

Those who do not keep a close eye on its development will be missing out on one of the most exciting innovation centers of the world.

Those who dismiss it will be downplaying the innovation willpower of 1 billion people.

And those who fear it will be forced to face it when Chinese AI propels humanity into a new world.

I wrote the following blog post to process what I ultimately saw as the rise of China in late 2018. I got many things right.

Sep 4, 2018

Why Peak Valley Got It Wrong

https://thetaklo.medium.com/why-peak-valley-got-it-wrong-3cdb82cbd171

The Economist recently published an article titled "Peak Valley." Fred Wilson addressed this post in his blog as well. My Zeroth partner Rodolfo also commented on his tweet.

There are two main points that Fred summarized that are to be addressed: the decline of the Valley in terms of innovation and the decline of global innovation. It's easier to look at each point separately.

The Decline of the Valley

There are three main elements of a healthy ecosystem, of which in my blog post I mentioned the free flow of human capital, intellectual capital, and financial capital. The Valley has been hampered because of more difficult immigration policies and rising cost of living, but this has been covered away by better financial capital flowing into the Valley, relative to anywhere else.

But no longer. Financial capital now can be deployed in startups anywhere in the world with more private and public capital available. The human capital friction that the Valley has still persists, so people are now choosing to stay in their home countries. And the intellectual capital available to build a startup is largely publicly available and decentralized.

Thus, this phenomenon isn't a decline of the Valley, but the relative rise of everywhere else.

The Decline of Global Innovation

*The relative rise of everywhere else
means that innovation can happen in
big cities like Shenzhen, London, Hong
Kong, or Tokyo, or small cities like Nairobi,
Amsterdam, or Wenzhou.*

*One evidence of this is the performance of
original apps and services that serve local
markets. For example, the Uber launch
in Hong Kong has not been successful
because it hasn't served local use cases,
but the local variant GoGoVan has gone
on to become a unicorn. Uber in mainland
China also didn't fare well against Didi, and
before arguing it is because of regulation
and protectionism, I would argue that those
two topics are extremely important parts of
localization; failure to address these risks is
a failure of localization, pure and simple.*

*Thus, the rise of everywhere else, or decen-
tralized innovation, should lead to more
global innovation.*

Linking it all together

What's funny though in the Economist *article is how the above two points are linked—a decline of Valley innovation equates to lessening innovation every-where—when clearly it should be decentralized innovation leads to more innovation. Either one has a bias toward Valley innovation as the end-all of innovation, or one disagrees with one of the premises I deconstructed above.*

Whichever way it is, I look forward to a future celebrating the rise of a decentralized rise of everywhere else.

I was right in the above: it *is* the relative rise of every-thing else, or as some call it, the multipolar world. This paradigm describes the rise of both China and India, so that now these nations including the US share the world stage in economic and political power.

As a technologist, I'm interested in witnessing the technological progress of these three distinct powers and the innovation they produce.

As an entrepreneurial advocate, I'm excited to see founders from these nations lead said innovation and unleash upon the world their visions.

And as a leader, I'm excited to interact with these founders and lead them through the age of AI.

Conclusion

WHEN I STARTED on the Zeroth journey a few years ago, I had a hypothesis of how things would turn out. The portfolio and the thesis outperformed, beyond my wildest dreams.

Looking back, I was very privileged. My LPs gave me a safe space to invest, understand, and work with brilliant founders. I enjoyed my time with all my Zeroth founders and learned from all of them; I always supported their journeys and always will. My utmost belief is that when founders succeed and become the best version of themselves, the returns will come.

I will always be creating new structures and exploring new horizons. That is what I do best, my unique contribution to the world.

Scan the QR code to access links to the blog posts in this book, a list of 100 ChatGPT prompts from The Automated, and other free resources.

About the Author

TAK LO leads ideas.

Previously, he built the Nalu fund, which focuses on blockchain and crypto, the Zeroth fund, which invested in over 50 startups in artificial intelligence, and at over 60 startups in the technology space while at Techstars

He advises organizations and governmental agencies on how to capitalize on technology disruption and economic transformation. He was an Non-official Member of the Committee on Innovation, Technology, and Re-industrialization of Hong Kong, a member of the ESS Assessment panel under the Innovation and Technology Fund of Hong Kong, and on the subgroup on Smart Hospitals for the Hospital Authority for Hong Kong. He also advised the Estonian government on its e-residency program and spoke on a US Congressional Panel on Veterans Affairs.

Tak has been featured in global media including *Bloomberg*, *The Economist*, *Forbes*, and *MIT Technology Review*. He has been published by outlets including *SCMP*, *Techcrunch*, and *Coindesk*.

An established keynote speaker and guest expert, Tak has spoken at events including TEDx, Connected Capital, Human-Level AI Conference, and AI and Society.

Tak is also fourth-generation Hong Kong. He can often be seen eating at Luk Yu, his family and Hong Kong's oldest restaurant.

Acknowledgements

I THANK MY founders for working with me and entrusting your journeys to me. I learned vicariously through your ups and downs, and you are the inspiration for much of what I write here.

Secondly, I thank my Zeroth investors. You allowed me the opportunity to work with great founders and to be able to learn from them. Without you, I would not have this chance for learning.

I thank my London family for being the very first ecosystem I was a part of building. I was honored to be a part of the process of building what it is now.

I thank my Techstars family, who gave me a shot at learning from the best founders and making lifelong founder friends. I learned my craft with you.

I thank my military family for gifting me the lessons of grit, determination, and courage. I started with you as a boy and left as a man.

I thank the Tak Army for all their help, especially Richard Lloyd, Peng Fei Chen, and Malte Wagenbach for looking over my drafts and providing invaluable feedback.

I thank my editor Ray Sylvester and designer George Stevens for guiding me along this book journey. I couldn't have had two better pairs of hands.

Lastly, I thank my family for being my constant, through thick and thin:

My father, Sam Lo, and step mom, Sabrina Lo. Thank you, Dad, for your patience, and especially Ee Ee for being the rock not only for Dad, but for my and Tak-Ho's families.

My deceased mother, Nora Chien Lo, for giving me the two greatest gifts a man can have: life and strength.

Mei Kwin, my wife. Thank you for going on this journey of life with me, with its ups and downs. I know it hasn't been easy—and I thank you for trusting me.

My children, Vera-Nora and Ethan-Noah. Sapiens qui prospicit.

www.ingramcontent.com/pod-product-compliance
Lightning Source LLC
Chambersburg PA
CBHW061528310726
48972CB00008B/2371